Gracie Fairshaw

and the

Mysterious

Guest

D1078271

Gracie Fairshaw

and the

Mysterious Guest

Susan Brownrigg

uclanpublishing

Gracie Fairshaw and the Mysterious Guest is a uclanpublishing book

First published in Great Britain in 2020 by
uclanpublishing
University of Central Lancashire
Preston, PR1 2HE, UK

978-1-9129793-4-9

1 3 5 7 9 10 8 6 4 2

Set in 10/17pt Kingfisher by Toni Murtagh

A CIP catalogue record for this book is available from the British Library.

Printed and bound in Great Britain by Clays Ltd, Elcograf S.p.A.

For

Mum and Dad

Preface

Gracie Fairshaw and the Mysterious Guest is set in Blackpool, 1935.

Blackpool, on the Lancashire coast, has been Britain's most popular seaside resort since the 1800s.

It is most famous for the 158 metre high Blackpool Tower and the Blackpool Illuminations, a 6.2 mile series of lights along the seafront.

Every Autumn, the 'Lights' are turned on by a special guest at the Switch-On ceremony.

In 1935 they were turned on by Audrey Mosson, a fifteen-year-old girl from Blackpool.

Chapter One

The Majestic

Most folk only noticed one thing about Gracie Fairshaw, but she noticed everything about them. 'Come in,' said Mrs Yates the landlady, ushering the Fairshaws into The Majestic boarding house. Mrs Yates was dressed in a cheery lilac ensemble, but Gracie spotted dark shadows under her eyes and noticed that her skirt was a good size too big. Mrs Yates was not sleeping and had lost weight. The widow was still grieving.

'Sorry we're a bit late, George needed a wee,' said Ma, ruffling his blond hair. 'I had hoped he'd learn to control his bladder by now. He is nine after all!'

'Ma!' wailed George.

'Don't worry about it,' said Mrs Yates. 'Let's go into the

parlour to do the handover. You'll be wanting to get yourselves settled in as soon as possible after your journey.'

Gracie was glad to put her suitcase down; it weighed a tonne! She left it next to Ma's and George's in the hall and they all followed Mrs Yates.

The parlour was furnished, but without any knick-knacks to make the room feel homely. There were a couple of faded armchairs with lace antimacassars covering the worn patches, a battered round table, an empty display cabinet and an old piano. Gracie tried to picture their family photographs on the wall and Ma's shepherdess ornament on the mantelpiece. It wasn't easy. The Majestic didn't feel like it belonged to them yet.

George threw himself into one of the armchairs. Her younger brother seemed to have no such concerns.

'Don't get too comfy, lad,' said Mrs Yates. 'It's hard work running a boarding house, and your ma is going to need you both to help.' She smiled at Gracie, but her eyes were on her left arm, which ended just past her elbow. 'Don't look so worried, dear. Phyllis, my best maid, has agreed to stay on for the weekend. She'll show you the ropes.'

Gracie blushed. She wandered over to the bay window and peered out through a gap in the curtains at the dark street. Every house in the row seemed to be a boarding house too.

'You've explained to your guests that there may be a little

disruption?' asked Ma.

Gracie turned to see Mrs Yates place a hand on Ma's shoulder. 'Yes, I'm sorry I couldn't hold off the handover until after the Illuminations. These last few guests will be no bother. It will be like having an extended family for a few days.'

Gracie's stomach swirled at the thought of sharing her home with strangers. Strangers stared and made clumsy comments about her arm.

'I've told my regulars they can stay on 'til Sunday,' said Mrs Yates. 'They come every year for the lights, and these new Switch-On events are becoming very popular. It's only the second time there's been a guest of honour to press the button. We're lucky here in Blackpool that our season is so long. Next year you'll have guests staying right through October!'

'I've left you a few basics in the kitchen, 'til you get settled in. There's Eccles cakes, tea and a bottle of milk.' Mrs Yates pulled out a bunch of keys from her lilac cardigan pocket. 'Congratulations, Mrs Fairshaw! You are officially The Majestic's new landlady. I hope you will be as happy here as my husband and I were.'

'Oh, we will be,' said Ma. 'I just know it.'

***

Gracie leaned against the wall as Ma unlocked the door to their private quarters. She closed her eyes, picturing their old home. On the outside, their house looked like the hundreds of others in Milltown; a little brick terrace shrouded in thick smog. There was no greyness inside though, only colour and warmth, thanks to Ma's beautiful handmade cushions, curtains, quilts, throws and rag rugs. Gracie blinked away a tear at the thought of the new owners settling in and using them. Ma's words echoed in her mind – 'We'll travel light; The Majestic has everything we need.' – but it didn't have any of the things that mattered to Gracie. She'd miss the little park at the end of the street, her friends who understood that she sometimes struggled with new situations and the neighbour's cat that would rub its body against her legs every morning.

She shook off her memories at the sound of George dragging his suitcase down the short hallway. She picked up her own and followed him.

'I still can't believe you've poked holes into it!' said Gracie, grinning.

'I 'ad to,' replied George, undoing the catches. 'How else is Fred supposed to breathe?'

'In Milltown,' said Ma, as they entered the small kitchen. 'That was what we decided, wasn't it?'

'Fred's changed his mind! He wants to live in Blackpool too.' He lifted out his pet rat and stroked its dark fur. 'He fancies a bit of sea air.'

Ma laughed as she filled the kettle. 'I must be soft. Go on, take him into your room, George. We don't want the guests seeing him!'

'Fred can sleep in my case tonight,' said George, wrinkling his brow, 'but we'll have to get him a proper cage soon.'

They gathered around the kitchen table and waited for the kettle to boil. Ma put a teapot on the table and laid out three cups and saucers. She found the paper bag of Eccles cakes in the bread bin and put one for each of them on to a plate. George bit straight into his.

'I can't believe The Majestic is actually mine!' said Ma, pouring the tea. 'It's just as I remember. I had such lovely family holidays in Blackpool, and there's so much more to do nowadays. The beach is really close; you can paddle in the sea, ride on a donkey and build a sandcastle too. There's yummy seaside food – ice cream, candy floss and pink sticks of rock. Then there's the pier, the Open Air Baths and the Pleasure Beach fairground all on our doorstep . . . and the Tower, of course! I loved it here when I was a kid, and I'm sure you will too.'

Gracie's chest tightened. She lifted her teacup to hide her trembling bottom lip. How could she spoil Ma's delight by telling her she was worried that she was going to hate living in Blackpool?

***

'Ma's put some clothes in your room,' said George, pushing past Gracie as she came out of the bathroom the following morning. 'You're going to look so funny.'

Gracie sighed and went back to her bedroom. There was a

maid's outfit on her bed. She picked up the black dress first; the colour had faded and the short sleeves were a bit frayed. The white apron was yellowed and the pocket was torn on one edge. A hand-me-down, probably from Phyllis.

Gracie put the clothes on and looked in the mirror. The dress was too big, and just seemed to hang from her. She gave her wavy, bobbed hair a fresh brush, then pulled on her plimsolls. Gracie picked up the apron and went to the kitchen to ask Ma to help with the straps. She would have to practice so she could tie them easily herself.

'You look nice. Very smart,' said Ma, as Gracie entered the kitchen. She held her hand out to receive the apron.

'It's a bit loose,' said Gracie.

'You don't want it too tight to work in,' said Ma. She wrapped the apron around her waist and pulled the straps tight. 'There, perfect. The apron makes a real difference. Oh, but that pocket could do with fixing, couldn't it? I'll sew it tonight.'

Gracie rubbed at the dress's collar as she watched Ma drop a slice of lard into the frying pan on the electric stove. The counter was full of food; Ma had ordered enough bacon to feed an army, along with trays of eggs, strings of sausages, black pudding and catering-sized tins of baked beans – and not a scrap for the Fairshaws until breakfast service was finished.

'Why don't you collect the bowls,' said Ma, as she lowered some rashers into the hot fat. 'The guests should have finished their cornflakes by now.'

Gracie wiped her brow and took an empty tray to collect in the dirty plates. The smell of bacon and eggs would usually be a comforting one, but this morning it made her feel queasy.

She swung open the dining room door with her hip. The Majestic felt like an over-stuffed suitcase about to burst its locks. Gracie made her way across the room, swerving round the guests' chairs. Everywhere she looked, families were shovelling food into their mouths as though it was a race to finish breakfast first.

Gracie went over to introduce herself to the maid. Phyllis looked about three years older than Gracie, around seventeen. She had long, dark brown hair and curves that looked unhappily restrained in her black dress. Her apron was starched white and perfectly pressed.

'Have you waitressed before?' asked Phyllis, her brown eyes appraising Gracie's appearance.

Gracie shook her head.

'Good job Mrs Yates kept me on then,' said Phyllis, beaming. 'What about bed making?'

'I find a way to do most new things,' said Gracie, raising her chin.

The maid nodded, then suddenly swept up a cruet set from the sideboard and passed it to a woman around Ma's age with surprisingly grey hair.

The woman took a pencil from behind her ear and jotted

down something in the notebook she had secreted on her lap. Gracie desperately wanted to know what she had written. She was convinced the guest was making notes about The Majestic. It made her uneasy.

The door into the kitchen opened and George sauntered in with half a sausage in his mouth. Gracie giggled and beckoned him over. 'Does Ma know you've got that?'

George chewed down the last of the sausage. 'It was a bit burnt, still tastes good though.'

'Well don't be pinching any leftovers off people's plates,' said Gracie. 'We're supposed to wait for our breakfast, remember?'

'I'm really looking forward to the Illuminations, aren't you?' asked Phyllis when Gracie returned.

'I think we'll be too busy to see the lights,' replied Gracie.

'Oh, but you must! I've been telling all the guests about them. They're using over 300,000 bulbs – or lamps – this year, lots of coloured ones too, according to the Gazette.'

'Oh,' said Gracie. 'That does sound a lot.'

'My favourites are the animated tableaux. 'Course you have to go all the way up to the North Shore cliffs to see them.'

Gracie looked blankly at her.

'They're big pictures made up of lights that move,' she explained. 'But if you want to stay nearer to home, the Pleasure Beach is to be lit up in neon. We could go together if you fancy it?'

'No, thanks. Won't it be very crowded?' Gracie shuddered as

she imagined faceless crowds. Thousands of strangers pouring out on to the Golden Mile; smothering the promenade, the beaches and Blackpool's three piers.

'Well, you're not going to like living in Blackpool if you don't like crowds!' scoffed Phyllis.

'Blimey O'Riley!' exclaimed George.

Gracie turned to see a glamourous couple enter the room. She was glad for the distraction and led them to a table. They were only just in time for breakfast.

The dark-haired man wore an expression as sombre as his suit. The blonde woman wore dark sunglasses and gritted teeth.

Gracie felt the man's eyes bore into her. Had she been staring at them for too long? They seemed far too posh to be staying in The Majestic.

'You're new,' he said.

'My mother has taken over The Majestic,' replied Gracie.

'Your mother?' Understanding dawned on his face, and his eyes widened. 'Ah yes, Mrs Yates mentioned something about new owners . . .' he smiled. 'Well, let's hope her breakfasts are as good.'

'Yes, sir. Would either of you like a drink first?'

'Nothing for me,' mumbled the woman.

'My wife will have a black coffee and a tea for me, please.'

'We'd like more tea, too,' called out one of the elderly twin sisters on the adjacent table.

'If you can manage with your arm,' said the other, peering over her glasses.

Gracie felt her cheeks burn up. She backed away from the table. She could feel everyone's eyes on her. Their expressions were the usual mixture of discomfort, pity and sympathy.

Gracie went to the side to pour their drinks. Her hand was shaking as she lifted the coffee pot.

'Mr Dixon has that effect on me, too,' said Phyllis. 'I think he looks just like that Hollywood actor, oh, you know who I mean ... Clark Gable.'

''E's got a moustache,' said George, rolling his eyes, 'that's all.'

'Make yourself useful and tell Ma there's two more for breakfast,' said Gracie.

'I'll take those drinks,' said Phyllis.

Most of the other guests had already left. There was just one more family in the dining room. The husband and wife were taking it in turns to persuade their little girl to eat her cereal. It was taking a long time.

'I suppose your ma will be making lots of changes now she's taken over The Majestic,' said Phyllis.

'What? Oh yes,' said Gracie. 'I suppose we might.'

'You should chuck out that piano. It's so old-fashioned. Happen you could get a Decca gramophone or a wireless.'

'Hmm, it'd be nice for guests to be able to listen t' latest dance bands,' agreed Gracie.

'Also, don't get me started on that wallpaper,' Phyllis sighed, looking at the beige floral print. 'I mean, *really*. It's practically Victorian! I think a nice, fashionable geometric pattern would be better.'

'I'm not sure if we can afford . . .'

'Well, it won't cost owt to get rid of that!' Phyllis pointed at a house rules sign hanging on the wall.

Guests must refrain from noise when rising.
Children must refrain from playing on the stairs and landing.
Children must refrain from playing the communal piano.

There was a sudden crashing sound. Gracie span around to see Ma standing in the doorway. Two upturned plates of breakfast lay on the floor.

'You'll have to add new carpet to your list,' said Phyllis.

Ma was staring into the dining room. Her face was as pale as egg white.

Chapter Two
The Vanishing Lady

Gracie rushed forward, Phyllis at her side.

Mr Dixon called out. 'Can we help?'

Ma started backing up into the little kitchen, her eyes unblinking.

'We're fine, Mr Dixon. We're just going to make you a fresh breakfast,' said Phyllis.

'I didn't want anything anyway,' reminded his wife.

'Nonsense,' replied Mr Dixon. 'We've got a big weekend ahead.'

'George, fetch a dustpan,' called Gracie. 'Don't worry, Ma. We'll get this cleaned up.' She could feel heat rising up the back of her neck. She was sure the guests were all watching her.

'Your ma looks a bit faint,' said Phyllis, as George appeared with a long-handled brush and a dustbin lid.

Gracie took Ma's arm and guided her into their private quarters. 'Let's sit you down.'

'Sorry, sweetheart. I just had a bit of a shock. It was one of the guests . . .' Ma shook her head as she settled on the settee. 'I was surprised to see them.'

'Who do you mean?' asked Gracie. She tried to recall who had been in the dining room. There'd been the two elderly sisters, the woman with the notebook, the Dixons and the young family with the little girl.

'They'll be leaving on Sunday any road,' said Ma, almost to herself. 'I doubt they even recognised me. Now how about a nice cup of tea for your ma? I don't know about you, but I could do with one.'

Gracie put her hand on Ma's arm. 'Are you sure everything's fine? You gave me a fright.'

Ma put on a smile. 'It's nothing. I just noticed someone I fell out with a long time ago. No, everything is splendid. I promise. You are happy we moved here, aren't you Gracie? I know you were settled in Milltown, but now you've left school we have to think about your future.'

Gracie lowered her voice. 'I do understand it's harder for a girl like me to find a job.'

'You can do anything you want,' said Ma. 'I knew that as soon as I saw you clambering out of your crib when you were just a babe. You've always found a way to manage. You're amazing

Gracie Fairshaw. I want the best for you and George, and I believe we'll have that here in Blackpool. I couldn't have either of you working in that mill. It's much too dangerous and that air was no good for your brother. It worried me the way he was wheezing.'

'He sounds better already,' said Gracie, gazing lovingly at her Ma. 'We will be happy here. Now, shall I go and fetch you that cuppa?'

Ma nodded. 'Good girl.'

But as Gracie walked towards the kitchen, she distinctly heard Ma sigh.

***

'Hey, daydreamer, your boiled egg is getting cold,' said Ma an hour later as they were sitting down to their own breakfast.

'I'm not sure I want it now.' Gracie was still worried about Ma. She seemed brighter, but still. *What had made her drop that tray?* She knew better than to question Ma too soon. She'd wait until she seemed more relaxed and then ask her about the mysterious guest again. Gracie couldn't imagine Ma falling out with anyone. *Which of the regulars could it have been?* thought Gracie.

'I'll eat your egg,' said George, reaching out for it.

Gracie tossed it to him. 'Phyllis suggested us older children should have bacon and eggs same as t' grown-ups. What do you think, Ma?' She nibbled on a piece of toast.

'Hmm, maybe. We'd have to charge more though.'

George started hammering at the top of his new egg with his teaspoon. 'I love dippy eggs and soldiers.'

'That's because you're nine – and I keep telling you, use your knife to slice the top off,' said Gracie.

Instead he pulled a shiny new penknife out of his shorts' pocket.

'Where on earth did you get that?!' exclaimed Ma, as he stabbed it into his egg.

'Found it,' George replied with a shrug, before he thrust it in again, causing a jet of yolk to shoot into the air.

'Put it away, George, before I confiscate it,' said Ma.

Gracie wiped her buttery fingers on the tablecloth. 'Phyllis is like a whippet fetching in those dirty dishes, and she dries much faster than I can wash. I think she's worried we won't keep her on. She's gone to make the beds already, and then she said she'll fetch those supplies you wanted. She's a proper workhorse.'

'I think we make a good team, don't you?' said Ma. 'Speaking of washing – look at the back of your neck, George!' She pulled out her handkerchief and licked the corner. 'Come here! You could grow potatoes in that muck! You were supposed to *use* that new soap I put out on t' basin for you. You'll have to have a bath tonight.'

'It's not even Sunday,' moaned George.

'Your rat stinks too,' said Gracie. 'We should give him a bath an' all, before the guests smell him!'

'We could all do with a bit of fresh air,' said Ma. 'How about a quick stroll down the prom? We've plenty of time before we have to do any laundry and prep for dinner. Let's get our coats.'

They went into the hall. Ma had a faraway look on her face as she pulled on her coat. She tutted at a loose button. 'Hmm, it should hold for now, but I'll sew it on tighter when we get back,' said Ma.

Gracie slipped her coat on over her maid's outfit. Ma had shortened the coat sleeves to make it more practical. Back in Milltown she'd made extra money doing sewing jobs for neighbours.

Ma stepped forward. 'Let me do you up,' she said, reaching out for the buttons.

'I can manage,' said Gracie.

Ma pulled back, feeling embarrassed. 'Of course you can.'

'You're not dressing me either,' said George.

Gracie looked him up and down and laughed. He had odd socks on, and his collar and tie were all skew-whiff. 'Where's your coat?'

George held up a dirty raincoat.

'You should wear it in the bath,' said Gracie, 'it could do with a clean too.'

'Oh, before I forget, here's a front door key of your own,' said Ma. The key was on a long loop of string. Gracie lifted it over her head.

Ma adjusted her cloche hat. 'Ready?'

Gracie and George nodded.

'Wait a minute, what's that?' She reached out behind George's ear and pulled out a coin. 'Well I never, look! A penny! How did that get there?'

'Is it for me?' asked George.

'Must be,' said Ma. She winked at Gracie and reached behind her ear. 'Well I never! There's one for your sister, too.'

'We can get some sweets,' said George. 'There's a paper shop on the corner, but it were shut last night.'

'Is there really?' said Ma. 'Let's pop in on our way to the seafront.'

They made their way through The Majestic, but at the front door Ma stopped abruptly and began to rummage through her handbag. 'I've only gone and forgotten me glasses.' She shook her head. 'I won't be a minute. Wait in there for me.'

Gracie pulled George into the parlour and they flopped down into the armchairs.

'What does she need her specs for, any road?' asked George.

'So she can keep an eye on you,' teased Gracie.

Gracie watched the minute hand on the grandfather clock rotate slowly, while George drummed his fingers on the armrest.

After about ten minutes, she stood up and opened the parlour door. George followed.

They peered along the corridor, looking for signs of Ma.

'Can we get a bucket and spade?' asked George, as a boy about his age passed by swinging a set.

'Maybe,' Gracie replied, distracted. 'Come on, let's hurry Ma up.'

They sprinted down the corridor to discover that the door to their private quarters was wide open. Something was lying on the floor.

As they got nearer, Gracie realised it was Ma's hat. That was strange.

She picked it up. The hat had been trodden on and the feather was all limp. It was rather old-fashioned, and she had wished for some time that Ma would stop wearing it. She certainly wouldn't be able to wear it now.

What was it doing on the floor?

'Ma?' Gracie and George stepped into their small hall. She wasn't in the kitchen or the dining room.

Gracie knocked on Ma's bedroom door. When there was no reply, Gracie opened it.

Ma's handbag was on the floor too; its contents spilt out.

Gracie felt her breakfast slide around in her stomach.

Something was wrong, she knew it.

Where had Ma gone?

Chapter Three
Surprise On The Sands

'**M**a! Where are you?' called Gracie. There was no reply. 'Here George, hold her hat. See if you can get the shape back.' She bent down and began to scoop Ma's things into the handbag; her compact, pen, even her reading glasses – but there was no sign of The Majestic's keys or her purse.

George posed in front of the mirror with Ma's hat on. 'Nah, it's no good. It's ruined.' He threw it on to the dressing table.

'Ma might have fainted, like she nearly did this morning,' said Gracie, taking a deep breath. They checked the bedrooms together, then the bathroom, but Ma wasn't there.

'We need to search the rest of The Majestic. Come on, George.'

'Hold on.' He grabbed his toothbrush glass. 'We can listen through doors with this.'

An open door and a forgotten hat weren't exactly fired gun shots and a pool of blood, but Gracie couldn't shake off the feeling that something bad had happened to Ma.

She walked quickly, her heart fluttering as they left their private quarters. 'Ma might have eaten something that disagreed with her – those sausages maybe?'

'Urrggh, not the runs,' George said squirming. 'Will I get them an' all?'

'Not you, you have a cast iron stomach!' said Gracie, trying to keep her tone reassuring. Her own tummy felt funny, but she knew this was just nerves. 'We'd best check the communal toilets.'

They headed into the guests' corridor and knocked on the toilet door.

There was a groan from inside.

'Ma, is that you? Are you all right?' whispered Gracie.

The voice moaned again.

'Ma! Let me in,' said Gracie, trying the handle – but it was locked. 'I'm really worried about you.'

The door handle suddenly dropped, and Gracie pulled it towards her.

It wasn't Ma.

'You'll have to flush it again,' said Mrs Dixon, wiping her mouth.

Gracie and George stepped back so the woman could pass.

There was a lingering smell of vomit. Gracie yanked the toilet chain again and led George to the reception nook at the other end of the hall.

The Majestic's public areas included all the bedrooms, the dining room, the guests' parlour and a public bathroom on each floor.

Gracie picked up the register. 'We need to be systematic.'

'Sistermatic?' questioned George.

'It means we need to check everything in a strict order to make sure we don't overlook anything.'

The Majestic had two almost identical floors of guests' rooms. They started on the top floor, searching along the corridor on the left. Here were two adjoining rooms; number five was Edna Hill and number seven was Elspeth Hill.

Gracie hooked the guest book under her left armpit and knocked on Edna's door.

'Come in.'

Gracie held a finger to her lips and indicated for George to wait in the corridor. She opened the door and stepped inside. 'Good morning, Miss Hill.' Gracie smiled. 'I am just checking all our guests are comfortable. Is there anything you require?'

It was her first time inside a guest's room. It was bigger than she'd expected and simply furnished with a bed, dressing table, chest of drawers, wardrobe and a small wash basin.

'You can't see my necklace, can you?' Edna pushed her glasses up her nose. 'It's gold with a large sapphire pendant. My sister *says* she hasn't borrowed it . . .'

Gracie looked on top of the dressing table. There was a hairbrush and mirror set with tortoiseshell handles, an Agatha Christie novel and an open ebony jewellery box containing a pair of diamond drop earrings. 'I can't, sorry. Shall I check under your bed?'

'Oh, do you think you could manage? I can't, not at my age. I'm eighty-three you know.'

Gracie crouched down and reached under the bed with her right arm. 'It's not there either.'

'Then Elspeth *must* have borrowed it.' She got up and knocked on the adjoining door.

Elspeth opened her door, revealing a room the mirror image of her sister's. 'I can hear every word you say, you know.' She shook her head at Gracie. 'I haven't got your necklace.'

'Check under her bed.'

'It will be that clasp, I told you to get it fixed. You could have lost that necklace anywhere, but it certainly isn't here, Edna.'

'Well, I'd best check in on the other guests,' said Gracie, retreating. Ma clearly wasn't in either room.

She closed the door.

'There's nobody int' bathroom,' said George.

They worked their way back along the other side of the floor. The room opposite Elspeth Hill's – number eight – was vacant.

Gracie tried the handle and the door opened.

The room was bigger than the sisters' and had twin beds. No sign of Ma.

George checked in the wardrobe as though it was a game of hide and seek.

They moved on to the last room, number six – the one occupied by the family with the little girl – the Barkers she presumed from the guest signing-in book.

She knocked and turned the handle.

'Oh! Sorry, Phyllis. We didn't know you were in here?'

'The Barkers asked me for another blanket. Your ma won't mind, will she? Some landladies are awfully strict about extras.'

'No, that's fine,' said Gracie.

'Have you seen our ma?' asked George.

Phyllis shook her head. 'I suppose Milltown children are not used to a big house like this one. Lost already!'

Gracie smiled, then pulled George out of the room before he said anything. She didn't want the maid thinking they couldn't look after themselves.

Downstairs was next. Gracie and George started on the right-hand side this time.

The first room, number two, belonged to the Fishwicks – the bucket and spade boy's family. She knocked again, and George used his glass trick. *They must have gone out too,* thought Gracie. Landladies were expected to turf guests out after breakfast, so it wasn't surprising most of the regulars weren't in.

Next was number four, Miss Steele's room. Gracie knocked – and tried the door. Miss Steele must have gone out and forgotten to lock it.

The room was a mess. There were notebooks everywhere; on the bed, on the floor and on top of the chest of drawers.

'I thought I was untidy,' said George, impressed.

Gracie flicked through a notebook while George peered over her shoulder. 'She's keeping notes on everyone staying in The Majestic,' she said, her mouth hanging open in surprise.

'*9 a.m. Mr Barker eats three rashers of bacon and a fried egg . . .*' George read. '*Dis – dis . . .*'

'Discusses,' said Gracie.

'*Discusses with wife plans for the day – he su – su . . .*'

'Suggests.'

'*A trip to the Winter Gardens,*' finished George. 'It's so boring!'

'This bit's funny though,' added Gracie, '*Mrs Barker is not keen. Her husband says the Empress Ballroom is superior to the Tower Ballroom. His wife says he's an idiot.*'

George groaned. 'We've found the world's most boring diary!'

Gracie pursed her lips as she silently read more entries. Edna Hill has two sausages for breakfast. Mr Fishwick played the piano in the parlour. Mrs Dixon had a glass of sherry in the parlour. 'I think you're right, George. Any road, one thing we do know is, Ma's not here. We should keep searching.'

They checked the communal bathroom, the separate toilet and then moved on to the other side of the corridor.

'George, check number one, the empty room,' said Gracie, as she knocked on number three, Mr and Mrs Dixon's room.

She could hear footsteps. After a minute, the door opened.

Mrs Dixon's blonde hair was still unbrushed and her face was all puffy. 'You again? What do you want now?'

Gracie winced. Her breath smelled awful. 'We're looking for our mother.'

'What's that got to do with me?' asked Mrs Dixon.

'She might be in your room,' said George, reappearing at Gracie's side and shaking his head.

'Well, she isn't.' She closed the door, muttering to herself.

George stuck out his tongue.

'Perhaps Ma has gone straight to the shop,' said Gracie, although it was funny that she'd left her handbag behind.

'Right, we check the paper shop first, and then the seafront.' Gracie put the guest book back in the reception nook. It bumped against something. She pulled it out. Another book.

LOST AND FOUND.

Gracie sniffed and blinked back a tear. Then she remembered Edna Hill's missing necklace. She turned back the cover and flicked through to find the last entry, so she could add it to the record.

She was surprised that there were so many missing

belongings, but then in a boarding house with people coming and going every week, it was probably normal for things to get mislaid. Plus, the book went back years. She wondered where Mrs Yates kept the found items – and if any had been returned to their rightful owners. Did she post strange parcels containing forgotten umbrellas or mislaid earrings across Lancashire and beyond?

Gracie found a pen on the shelf and added the sapphire necklace to the book. Her gaze fell on the opposite page where Mr Barker had reported a lost silver cigarette case. She'd mention both to Phyllis; after all, the maid was most likely to find them.

***

Gracie and George went straight down Osborne Road to the seafront. There were a few folk heading the same way. Gracie scanned them all in the hope that one was Ma.

It was like everything was happening in slow motion. Gracie was overly aware of everything, as though this moment would be for ever in her memories as the day Ma disappeared.

They stopped off at the small row of shops, but Ma wasn't in the paper shop or the laundrette – and the chip shop wasn't even open yet.

George clasped Gracie's hand as they made their way to the beach. 'We will find her, won't we?'

She blinked away threatening tears. What if they couldn't?

Would they have to go to the police?

George's expression changed. 'Has summat awful happened to Ma? Tell me!'

'Don't be silly. Let's keep walking.'

The South Shore stretched across ahead of them. Horses pulling carts trotted past. Families giggled and pointed out to sea.

Opposite was the impressive Open Air Baths – and to the left – the beautiful white casino building with its pretty oriental turrets.

Gracie swept her hair out of her eyes with a quick flick of her fingers as she waited for a tram to jingle past, then they dashed across the lines to the paved esplanade. She gazed out at the beach and the Irish Sea beyond. There were dozens of people already on the sand. *Could one of them be Ma?*

George let go of Gracie's hand. 'I'll find her,' he called, sprinting away.

'Stop!' she cried. 'Wait for me!'

Her brother ran on, down the steps and on to the sands.

Gracie cursed and darted after him. She could feel folk's eyes burning into her as she shouted his name.

'Ma, Ma!' called George, as he weaved frantically up and down the beach, grabbing at anyone who looked a bit like her.

Gracie waved her arms to try and catch his attention, but it was hopeless. She chased after him, her feet losing their grip on the shifting sands. She reddened as tourists stared at her, as though she was responsible for her brother's behaviour – just because she was older.

Then, suddenly, George was flat down on the ground. Gracie squealed and rushed towards him.

He had tripped over what appeared to be a large mound of sand.

George got up. Luckily, he didn't look hurt.

'You idiot!' shouted a voice. 'Why don't you look where you're going?'

Gracie looked down at the mound and realised there was a head sticking out of one end. She tried to catch her breath from running. She felt all hot and bothered, so she undid her coat buttons.

The buried boy had tanned skin and russet hair. He was about Gracie's age. His face was covered in a dusting of sand. He spat a mouthful out and laughed. 'Give us a hand, then,' he said, wriggling so that cracks appeared in the mound.

Gracie shrugged off her coat, letting it fall to the ground. She stretched out her right arm.

'Not like that – dig.' The boy stopped short. 'Oh, oh,' he said, staring.

'You heard him, George,' said Gracie, kneeling down to help.

'I didn't see, I didn't realise,' stuttered the boy.

George stiffened. 'Better half an arm than half a brain.'

Gracie shook her head. 'You didn't mean any offence,' she said, scooping up the sand. George began to dig too.

After a few minutes and more squirming, the boy was able to free himself. He stood up and stretched. 'Thanks,' he said, shaking Gracie's hand, then George's. 'I could have been there all day!'

Gracie brushed the sand off her knees and left elbow.

'What happened to the rest of your arm?' asked the boy, pointing.

Gracie swallowed. 'Shark bit it off.'

The boy's mouth fell open.

Gracie folded her arms; the shorter one to the front. 'I was born like this, and folk have been gawping and asking questions ever since.'

The boy blushed and looked to her eyes instead. She noticed he had friendly eyes – blue and twinkly. She felt sorry for snapping.

'You here on your holidays, then?' asked the boy.

George rubbed his ankle. 'We've got to be going. Come on, Gracie.'

'I'm Tom, by the way.' The boy smiled. It was a nice smile.

'Buzz off, Tom,' said George. 'We've got important business.'

'So, let me help. Members of the League of the Shining Star are always ready to assist.'

'Sorry, but we haven't time to hear about your League of

the whatsit,' said Gracie, edging backwards. 'We're looking for our ma.'

'Ma!' called George again. 'Where are you, Ma?'

'Are you lost?' Tom scanned up and down the beach. 'Don't fret. Your ma can't be far away. What's she wearing?'

Gracie sighed. She may as well give a description, though she knew it was pointless. Finding Ma among so many people was like looking for a needle in a haystack. 'She has wavy light brown hair and blue eyes, like me. She's not very tall, she's slim.'

'Very pretty, too,' added George.

Gracie smiled at him. 'She's wearing a blue checked dress with a belt, but she's got her green raincoat on over the top.'

'She's no hat on,' added George. 'She left it behind with her handbag.'

'Her hat *and* handbag?' repeated Tom. His mouth was set hard. 'A respectable woman like your mother would never go out without her hat and handbag.' He paused, placing a hand on Gracie's shoulder. 'Tell me everything that's happened, from the beginning.'

Chapter Four

The Conjurer's Cabinet

'She's been snatched,' said Tom, after Gracie recapped how they had found out Ma was missing. 'It's obvious.'

'Snatched?' repeated Gracie. It sounded far-fetched, like something from one of those James Cagney gangster movies that her brother was always asking to see.

'Who'd want to take Ma?' asked George.

'Good question,' said Tom. 'You said she talked about recognising someone, someone she'd argued with some time ago?'

'That's right,' said Gracie, 'but she didn't say who it was.'

'People generally disappear for one of two reasons,' Tom continued. 'The first is kidnapping. Are your parents rich?'

George guffawed. 'We're from Milltown!'

'We don't live with our pa,' said Gracie, quietly. 'He met another woman and moved to Wales with her. Ma had some savings put aside for the deposit and she's taken out something called a mortgage.'

'So, there's no one to pay a ransom – and there was no note, I presume, or you would have mentioned it.'

Gracie shook her head. 'What's the second reason people vanish?' she asked, her voice trembling.

'Because somebody wants them out of the way; maybe they've seen or heard something they shouldn't. Either way, time is against us. If we're to rescue your ma – we need to work fast.'

'I think we should tell the police,' said Gracie.

George gasped.

Tom shook his head. 'They'd never listen to a bunch of kids and you don't want to make the kidnapper angry.'

'You've got to come to The Majestic,' said George, tugging on Tom's jacket. 'Help us work out which one of the guests has Ma.'

Tom smiled, 'Lead the way.'

Gracie realised he was teasing them. Tom didn't believe their story at all. He thought he would find Ma back at their boarding house and be able to claim the mystery solved.

Gracie hesitated, then hurried after the boys. She desperately wanted Tom's ending to come true. Besides, if Ma was at The Majestic, she would be furious that Gracie had let George run off with a stranger – even if this one did have friendly eyes and a nice smile.

She sped past the deckchairs and caught up with Tom and George. The boys had stopped, their path blocked by a tall girl in a pale yellow swimming costume and a matching bathing cap. The girl's golden skin was all goose pimply.

'Oh no,' moaned Tom. 'Don't say owt. If our Violet finds out what we're up to she'll want to come an' all.'

Violet looked like a stretched version of Tom. She could only be his sister. 'If I find out what? That you've freed yourself? I can see that, stupid.'

'I had to, otherwise I'd've drowned.'

'Don't be a baby, Tom Emberton! I only nipped to t' loo. I don't wee in the sea like you!'

George guffawed. 'Wee in the sea,' he sang. 'Wee in the sea.'

'You must be freezing,' said Gracie.

Violet shrugged. 'The cold don't bother me. One day I want to swim the Channel. I practice every day, whatever the weather. Tom makes me pack him into the sand, so he can stay warm. He's more . . . doggy paddle.' Her gaze was on Gracie's elbow. 'Do you swim?'

'Yes.' The public baths were popular in Milltown. You could do a few lengths and get a hot shower after, which was better than waiting your turn for the old tub in front of the kitchen fire.

'Tell her about the shark,' said George.

Gracie ignored him.

'How old are you? I'm fourteen,' said Violet.

'I'm fourteen an' all!'

'Do you want to hang out on the beach with me? There are loads of older boys about,' said Violet, pulling off her cap to reveal her long, auburn hair. 'We could have a splash about in t' sea, or we could go to the Open Air Baths, if you prefer?'

'Sorry, can't. We're going to . . .' Gracie swallowed the rest of her words.

Violet grabbed her brother's arm and yanked it behind his back. 'You better tell me what you're up to. Confess.'

'Ow! Geroff Vi! All right, all right.'

His sister released him. Gracie wondered if it had been wise to turn down her invitation. She was scary.

'I'm helping Gracie and George,' said Tom. 'Their ma's vanished.'

'Vanished?' Violet reached out for his arm again. 'Tell me what you're really doing, or else.'

'He's telling the truth,' said Gracie. 'Our ma's disappeared. We're going back to our boarding house to work out who's snatched her and get her back.'

Violet stared into Gracie's eyes. 'OK, I believe you. At least, I believe that you think she's been taken. Personally, I wouldn't listen to my little brother – he's a bit thick. I, on the other hand, have intelligence *and* looks.'

'You're only ten months older,' whined Tom. 'Besides, this has nothing to do with you, Vi'.'

'Ha! Like I'm going to let you go chasing after villains without me. What would Pa say? He's already cross about me pinching his pliers. He'll be furious if you get mixed up in a kidnapping. Wait there while I get me clothes.'

'Pliers?' asked Gracie, once Violet was out of earshot. She couldn't imagine a girl wanting to borrow a man's tools.

'Violet likes to work out how things work; she's forever taking things apart so she can fathom them. She's pretty good at it an' all. Pa doesn't like it though – he thinks girls should be girls and boys should be boys. Violet says the world's changing. "Look at Amelia Earhart",' she says. I think she'd like to be a pilot herself when she's older, or an engineer at least.'

'What about you?' asked Gracie.

'Me?' replied Tom.

'What do you want to be? Who's your hero?'

'Promise you won't laugh . . .'

''Course not,' said Gracie. 'Go on, I swear.'

'Fred,' said Tom.

George gasped. 'How do you know my Fred?'

Gracie clapped her hand over her eyes. 'He doesn't mean your blooming rat, silly.'

'Oh,' said George, disappointed. 'Which Fred do you mean?'

'There's only one Fred in my book, no offence George,' said Tom, breaking into a short tap dance. 'Astaire!'

Gracie was going to ask if he'd seen the film *Top Hat* yet, when Tom stopped his routine short. Violet was back, dressed in corduroy dungarees and a double-breasted red coat; a matching beret pulled over her damp hair. She adjusted the man's watch on her wrist. 'So, tell me Gracie. Have you seen anyone acting suspiciously?'

'Hmm,' said Gracie. 'There was one person behaving strangely at breakfast. A woman called Miss Steele was writing everything down in a notebook. We found loads of other notebooks in her room later when we were looking for Ma.'

'Has this Miss Steele got a tape measure? You know – for checking out the size of rooms? Folk buying property are always trying to work out square footage,' said Violet. 'Could be she's a deranged property developer who wants the land The Majestic's built on.'

'She seems more interested in the guests,' replied Gracie.

'Hmm,' said Tom. 'Bet she's calculating how many people she can squeeze in. She'll be thinking of her profit line.'

'I'm wondering if she's summat to do with the local council,' said Violet.

'We should make a list of suspects – and put Miss Steele at the top of it,' said Tom.

Gracie nodded. *Could Miss Steele have kidnapped Ma?* she thought. *They were about the same age. Was she the person Ma had fallen out with? Were they friends turned enemies?* She shuddered as a picture of the grey-haired woman with a hand clasped tightly over Ma's mouth formed in her mind.

Violet looped her arm round Gracie's left one. 'Come on, daydreamer, we won't find any more clues here.'

They ran up the steps and across the promenade on to Osborne Road. They raced past the launderette with its smell of soapy washing and then past the paper shop, before halting by the chip shop.

A large van marked: *Tower Removals* was parked in front of The Majestic.

'Talk about jumping in your grave!' said Tom. 'Looks like Miss Steele's moving you out already.'

Gracie pulled free from Violet and dashed across the road. She could sense George and the others on her heels.

At the boarding house gate, Gracie bent down pretending to fasten her shoelace. She'd used the technique before; folk often looked away when they saw her struggling. They never even noticed her shoes were plimsolls.

George, Tom and Violet leant against the boarding house wall.

The front door opened, and Mr Dixon strode furiously towards the van.

Gracie swivelled around to see what was happening.

Two men in overalls and flat caps got out. 'Mr Dixon?' asked the driver. 'Mr Reginald Dixon?'

His mate sniggered.

Tom suddenly started coughing. Gracie turned to see him tugging on his ear.

She pretended to be fixing her other shoe and shuffled back a little, so she could listen for longer.

'You're late,' spat Mr Dixon.

The driver puffed out his cheeks. 'Well, you haven't been in any hurry to pay. Six months this lot's been in storage – and we don't unload until you cough up.'

Mr Dixon reached into his coat and pulled out a thick wad of notes.

George gave a whistle.

'Shh,' whispered Gracie.

The driver counted the money.

'It's all there,' said Mr Dixon. 'I came into some cash.'

The driver's mate grunted. 'Not like you to have money! You won't mind if I check the notes? Don't want you pulling any tricks.'

'If there's any damage to my equipment . . .' warned Mr Dixon. 'I've got a very important show tomorrow.'

The driver grunted and unhooked the back shutter.

Gracie twisted her head to get a clearer look. She gasped; the van was filled with brightly coloured trunks painted with an image of a top hat and a magic wand. Baskets overflowed with coloured scarves, handkerchiefs and artificial flowers.

'Wow,' said George, pointing to a long cabinet decorated with the shape of a blonde-haired woman. 'You're a . . .'

Mr Dixon narrowed his eyes. 'Butcher.'

Gracie didn't think he was funny.

The men offloaded a carry case containing two white rabbits, a transport crate for doves, and a bird cage marked Sunny containing a pretty yellow budgie.

Mr Dixon was a conjurer!

He snatched the delivery note from the driver. 'The bulk of it can go to The Abracadabra. They've agreed to store it until Saturday's show, but I want you to unload the carpet bag and the big cabinet here – and the animals of course. Take them to the second room on the left, my wife will let you in.'

'It won't fit through that front door,' said the driver.

'It will if you turn it lengthways, idiot!' growled Mr Dixon. 'Get on with it.'

George pointed to a wicker basket with swords sticking out of it. 'How does that one work?'

'Get in it and I'll show you,' said Mr Dixon, narrowing his eyes.

'Oh no,' said Gracie. She didn't want her brother pierced like a giant pincushion. 'Did our ma say you could store conjuring equipment in your room?' The men were now lifting out a large saw that made a vibrating sound as it wobbled. 'Some of it looks quite dangerous.'

'I haven't had the pleasure of meeting your mother yet. No, this was all arranged before your family took over,' he said, running his hands around a set of large gold rings. 'Why, is there a problem?'

'No, no problem,' said Gracie, reaching for her front door key. 'Well, we'd better go in and help make dinner,' she added, trying to make her voice sound casual.

'I really thought it was a new buyer moving in,' said Gracie, once they were all safely inside the Fairshaw's private quarters. She felt like her heart was still in her mouth. She hung up their coats, then went to fetch Ma's handbag and squashed hat to show Violet and Tom.

'Reginald Dixon doesn't sound much like a conjurer's name, does it?' said George, as Gracie joined the others in the kitchen. 'I thought he'd be called something like – the Astounding Alphonse.'

'Well, obviously Reginald Dixon isn't his real name,' said Tom, as Gracie put the kettle on to boil.

Gracie scrunched up her nose. 'How can you be sure?'

'Because there's only one Reginald Dixon in Blackpool, silly! Surely you've heard of him? He plays the Blackpool Tower Wurlitzer organ.' Tom moved his fingers as though playing piano keys. 'Your Mr Dixon is using a pseudo – a what-do-you-call-it – a false name.'

'An alias,' said Gracie.

George rubbed his hands with glee. 'We've found the bad guy!'

Chapter Five
Dinner Is Served

'It could be a coincidence,' said Gracie, her ear to the door as she listened to the removal men dragging the cabinet upstairs. 'He *might* be called Reginald Dixon – there's a girl at school called Shirley Temple.'

'Gracie's right,' said Violet, 'but he's definitely on our list of suspects with Miss Steele either way. Now, remind me who was in the dining room?'

'Besides the Dixons and Miss Steele, there was me and George. Oh – and Phyllis the maid, but Ma had already met her the night before,' Gracie began, as she poured out the tea, 'and she's only a couple of years older than us. Then there's Edna and Elspeth Hill and the Barker family. Personally, I think it unlikely that any of those are the kidnappers. I can't see the old ladies snatching Ma, and the Barkers have a little girl.'

'We shouldn't rule anyone out until we have proof,' said Tom, spooning sugar into his cup. 'We need to search all the rooms properly.'

'The keys to any unoccupied rooms are kept in the reception nook,' said Gracie, 'and the guests have the other room keys. Phyllis the maid has a set for cleaning and Ma has a master set,' said Gracie, 'but they're not in her bag. The kidnapper may have taken them. I don't like the idea of someone being able to go wherever they like in The Majestic.'

'We could get all the locks changed, but that would be really expensive,' said Tom. 'We'll just have to be vigilant.'

'So, how will we search the rooms?' asked George. 'Will we have to break in?' he clapped with excitement.

'I reckon I could pick the locks,' said Violet with a shrug.

'Great...' The sound of footsteps approaching the room made Gracie stall. 'Who's that?' She jumped up. 'Ma?'

'It's me,' said Phyllis, stepping into the room with two bags of shopping. 'You won't believe what I've just seen! A van outside filled with conjuring equipment!'

'Didn't you know Mr Dixon was a conjurer, Phyllis?' asked Gracie, her eyebrows raised. 'He said Mrs Yates had given permission for him to store some of his equipment in his room.'

'News to me,' replied the maid, putting the bags down. 'I suppose he does look quite theatrical, and his wife is ever so glamorous.' She reached into her shoulder bag for her purse. 'Here's your ma's change. I got everything on her list.'

'Oh, thank you,' said Gracie, taking the coins.

Tom and Violet were staring at the maid, clearly assessing her guilt.

'My feet are killing me. Just in time for a cuppa I see, I'm spitting feathers!' said Phyllis, putting her bag under the table so she could take off her coat.

Gracie reached over for another cup.

'Aren't you going to introduce me to your friends?' asked the maid.

'This is Violet and Tom,' said George. 'They're helping us to find—'

'Our way around the kitchen,' Gracie interrupted. 'Ma had to go out, something to do with the bank. We said we'd make dinner. There are only a few guests to feed after all.'

'You two know how to cook?' Phyllis looked unconvinced. 'Well, try not to burn the place down. I'm going to lay the tables.'

Gracie let out her breath once the maid had gone into the dining room. 'I don't think we should tell Phyllis that Ma has vanished. Not until we're sure we can trust her.'

'I agree,' said Violet, 'she looks a bit shifty to me. Besides, we haven't time to explain everything – the guests will want their midday meal. What's on the menu?'

Gracie shrugged. 'I don't really know any recipes.'

'Cheese on toast?' suggested George. 'Or summat out of a tin?'

'A tin?!' cried Tom. 'I'll pretend you didn't say that. We're not going to lower ourselves to tins. How hard can cooking be? It always looks easy enough. You chop it up, stick it in a pan and the heat does the rest.'

'Pa does all the cooking since Ma died,' said Violet. 'Tom loves to watch him.'

'I'm sorry to hear about your ma,' said Gracie.

'Me too,' added George.

'Thank you,' said Violet. 'It was a long time ago, but we still miss her.'

'So, what's in the shopping bags?' asked Tom. 'Your ma must have had a particular dish in mind.'

Gracie began emptying out the contents. There were several packs of mince, some onions, potatoes and a few carrots.

'Is it lamb or beef?' asked Tom.

Gracie read the label. 'Lamb.'

'Hotpot it is. I'll need a big frying pan and two saucepans. Violet, you can peel those spuds and carrots. George, you do the bread and butter.'

'What shall I do?' asked Gracie.

'Oh, I'm not sure,' said Tom, his eyes darting. 'You could pass me those onions?'

Gracie handed a paper bag filled with extra-large white

onions. Tom placed them on the kitchen table and grabbed one. He then took a chopping knife and tried to peel off the outer skin, but it slipped out of his fingers and rolled on to the floor.

'It's ok, I've got it!' Tom picked the onion up. This time he placed his other hand firmly on top and began to cut.

The onion squirted juice into his eye. Tom squinted as tears began to run down his cheek.

'Don't cry,' said George. 'It's only an onion. It doesn't mind that we're going to fry it in hot fat.'

'Ow!' Tom cried out, dropping the knife and waving his finger in the air. A drop of blood fell on to the tabletop.

'Let me see,' Gracie leaned over. 'It's only a nick. Keep some pressure on it and it'll stop. Now, why don't you let me take over?'

'Go on,' said Violet. 'She can't be any worse than you.'

Gracie took a fresh onion out of the bag and held it in place firmly with her left elbow. Violet passed her a small paring knife. Carefully, Gracie sliced down the centre of the onion – cutting right through it.

Tom relaxed and started to look for a frying pan.

Gracie released the onion and turned one half flat side down. She held the onion with her elbow again and gently eased off the brown papery outer skin. Then, she slowly sliced the onion, before repeating the technique with the second half.

'Want to help me peel?' asked Violet.

Gracie grinned. 'Sure, after I've finished these.'

Once the potatoes and onions were ready for the pan, Tom dropped the spuds into a pan of boiling water, almost scalding himself.

'How high should the heat be?' he asked, pushing the onions into the hot frying pan.

The fat began to spit and smoke.

'Not that high,' said Violet. 'Turn it down, quick!'

The onions were turning black.

'What are you burning?' asked Phyllis, appearing at the kitchen door.

'Nothing,' replied everyone, wafting the air.

Violet passed Phyllis a tray of bread and butter. 'You'd better not keep the guests waiting. It won't be long.'

Tom pushed the mince into the pan. 'The meat will cool it all down.'

He pushed the raw meat round and round the pan with a wooden spoon. The lid on the potatoes rattled. His face was bright red; sweat dripping from his brow. 'Pa makes it look much easier,' he squeaked.

The noise from the dining room was getting louder. 'Sounds like they've polished off the bread and butter,' said Violet, eyes wide, 'and now they want flesh.'

Meanwhile, Tom had managed to flick chunks of mince everywhere. 'Can you smell burning?' he asked, turning down the mince.

'The spuds!' cried Gracie. 'Be careful.'

Tom lifted off the lid. The water had boiled away, and the spuds had stuck to the bottom. He shoved at them with his spoon, so they flew into the mince. They were black – and an acrid smell rose from the pan.

The door swung open. 'Is everything all right back here?' It was Miss Steele with her notebook.

Violet gasped. 'You're not a health inspector, are you?'

Miss Steele fanned her face. 'No, I'm not, but if I was, I'd shut you down.'

'It's just a bit messy in here,' said Tom. 'We just need five more minutes.'

'You need a miracle,' quipped Miss Steele. 'Your meat is raw, and your potatoes are practically charcoal.'

'They're a bit crispy,' said Tom, 'some people like them that way.'

'Where is the new landlady?' asked Miss Steele, looking around. 'Mrs Fairshaw isn't it? I can't believe she would leave you children in charge of the catering.'

'She's sick,' lied Gracie.

'Not something she ate I hope?' Miss Steele raised an eyebrow.

'Just a cold, she didn't want to spread her germs,' Gracie embellished.

'She's all snotty,' added George.

Miss Steele smiled. 'And you thought you'd save her from

worrying by making dinner, am I right?'

'Yes,' said Gracie, 'exactly.'

'You're not from Blackpool, are you?' asked Miss Steele. 'That's a Milltown accent isn't it? I should have known. Milltown children are very resilient and self-sufficient.' She turned to Tom. 'But you're very obviously Sandgrownuns. Whatever were you thinking, young man?' Miss Steele shook her head and laughed. 'I'll tell the other guests they should get their dinner at the chippy over the road. Your ma can arrange a refund when she's feeling better.'

***

'Thank goodness everyone's gone,' said Gracie, with a sigh of relief. 'I'm exhausted.'

'I should never have left you alone,' said Phyllis. 'I'd better check everyone's happy. You don't want to lose your regulars.'

'Thank you' said Gracie. 'That's very kind of you.'

'She's seems nice,' said Violet.

'Phyllis?' asked Gracie.

'Yes,' replied Violet.

'She could be pretending to be kind and helpful,' said Tom, 'but I agree, she's nicer than that rude Miss Steele.'

'I know,' said Violet. 'I'm from Blackpool and I'm very self-sufficient thank you!'

Gracie dropped to her knees and reached under the table, trying not to laugh.

'Let me get that onion,' said Tom, 'after all, I dropped it.'

'I'm not fishing for the onion,' said Gracie as she reached into Phyllis's bag. 'I'm after these.'

She jangled the maid's keys.

Chapter Six

Room For Doubt?

'I say we do this in pairs,' Violet checked her watch. It was unusually big and expensive looking. 'It's 12:45 pm. You boys can investigate upstairs. That means you need keys to rooms five, Edna, seven, Edith – and six, the Barkers.'

'We'll do the ground floor. That's two, the Fishwicks – three, the Dixons – and four, Miss Steele.'

'We need the keys back in Phyllis's bag pronto,' said Gracie. 'If anyone catches us, we say we're making the beds.' She held the key ring down on the table with her left elbow and wriggled off each key and corresponding fob so she could share them out.

'When you're done,' said Tom, 'meet us by the shops.'

'When *you're* done,' corrected Violet. 'We're bound to be quicker than you two.'

Gracie put her coat on and they wandered out into the guests' corridor. The girls watched the boys creep towards the stairs.

The girls turned left and knocked on Miss Steele's door. When there was no answer, she put the number four room key into the lock.

Gracie reached out for the door handle, her heart racing.

'Fingerprints,' said Violet. 'Use your apron so you don't leave any.'

Gracie gripped the door handle through the thin cotton material and twisted it. The door opened. 'Remind me to lock it afterwards,' she whispered.

The girls slipped inside.

The room looked just as it had earlier that morning. Total chaos.

'We will find my ma, won't we, Vi?' asked Gracie, as she examined the chest of drawers.

"Course we will,' replied Violet, her head poking into the wardrobe.

'You don't think the kidnappers have . . . hurt her?' Gracie asked quietly. She inhaled deeply through her nose, trying to stop herself from sobbing.

'No,' said Violet firmly, crossing the room and taking her hand, 'but they've probably got her tied her up, so she can't escape.'

Gracie pictured Ma fastened to a chair with a thick rope, a gag across her mouth. She shook the image away quickly.

They continued to search, but Miss Steele seemed to own only three identical grey skirt suits, some pretty underwear, a wash bag and other personal items, plus her notebooks and enough pens to open a stationery shop.

'We should get some scissors, in case it is the Dixons who have her,' said Violet examining some nail clippers. 'I bet conjurers do really good knots.'

Gracie nodded, 'George has a pen knife. We could use that.' She picked up another notebook and began to read.

5pm – Tomato soup and barm cakes for tea. Edna Hill has two bowlfuls. Elspeth has her barm cake with margarine, not butter.

'I think Miss Steele must have some sort of compulsion to write everything down,' said Gracie. 'It's like an obsession.'

'It really is tedious stuff, worse than Tom's diary!'

'Tom writes a diary?' asked Gracie, surprised.

Violet grinned. 'Don't tell him I know. He'll kill me.' She put the notebook down. 'Let's search the Dixons' room next.'

***

There was no answer across the corridor. This time Violet unlocked the door.

The Dixons' room was more like a magic shop than a bedroom!

There was conjuring equipment everywhere – cups, gold rings, playing cards and bits of rope. Violet held up a fake finger and pointed it at the upright conjurer's cabinet.

'Quick, help me get it open,' said Gracie. 'Ma, are you in there?'

There was no answer. Gracie knelt down and tried to work out how to open the cabinet.

The front was made up of three doors on top of each other. One from feet to waist, the next from waist to shoulders and the third for the head. Each had its own catch and keyhole. There were also two thin slots above and below the middle segment, for sharp blades to be pushed into.

She tried to poke her finger into a keyhole, but even her little finger wouldn't fit.

Violet had found the blades against the wall. 'Look, the handle is much wider than the actual blade. I bet that's part of the trick,' she said, before joining Gracie.

Gracie was just glad they hadn't been inserted into the cabinet. She flipped back each catch in turn. There were no handles or doorknobs – the idea was that the assistant would push open the cabinet from inside when it was time to reappear. Gracie carefully held on to a catch and gently pulled, hoping the doors weren't locked.

It began to lift. Violet took some of the weight and they opened the first catch fully –then the other two. But the cabinet was empty. There was no secret compartment.

Ma was not inside.

'Ah, I get it,' said Violet. 'The assistant must have to twist and squeeze to one side out of the reach of the blades. She is safe in that position because the blades are narrower than the box. The lady doesn't *really* get cut in half.'

The girls turned their attention to the animals. The doves cooed as Violet peered into their transport crate on top of the chest of drawers. The rabbits snuffled in their carry case next to them. They all looked perfectly ordinary.

Gracie wandered over to the dressing table and a covered bird cage. She peeled the material off to reveal a yellow budgie shaking its tail feathers.

'Hey Presto!' said the bird. 'The lady has re-appeared.'

Gracie swallowed. 'What did you say?'

The budgie began to chirp. The bird was pretty, but could he really hold any clues to Ma's disappearance?

'Hello, Sunny,' said Gracie.

The budgie gave a long whistle. 'Hello, Sunny.'

'It's mimicking you,' said Violet, coming closer.

'It's mimicking you,' copied Sunny.

'Sunny,' said Gracie gently. 'Where is the lady?'

He began to chirp again. 'Find the lady.'

'Yes,' said Gracie. 'That's right.'

'Hey Presto! Before your very eyes,' replied the budgie. 'The lady vanishes.'

'Yes, but where is she?' asked Violet, rattling the cage. 'Tell us, bird brain!'

'Hey Presto! For my next trick,' trilled Sunny, 'I shall saw the lady in half.'

'Shut up,' Gracie hissed, 'Shut up.' She threw the cover over the budgie, her hand shaking. She rubbed her forehead – there was a throbbing building in the middle of it.

They swivelled around to check under the twin beds.

'Watch out for snakes,' said Violet, as she and Gracie lay on the floor to look underneath. 'Conjurers always have snakes.'

The girls counted down together. 'Three, two, one,' and reached underneath. They patted around.

'Nothing,' they whispered. They blew out air in relief, before standing up again.

Gracie searched the chest of drawers. She patted down three pairs of folded underpants without fuss, while Violet pulled out the chamber pots from under the beds. Gracie knew plenty of girls that would have shuddered at the idea of this, even though the pots were unused. She liked the fact that Violet just got on with things, too.

Next, they checked the pillows on each bed. Gracie found a set of man's pyjamas tucked under one, while Violet pulled out a nightie and half a bottle of whisky from the other.

'I think Mrs Dixon has a drink problem,' she said.

Was that why she was sick earlier? thought Gracie. *How sad.*

She moved on to the wardrobe, the hinges squealing like a violin as she opened the door. Gracie searched through the rack of bright coloured costumes; they were short, low cut and covered in sparkles.

'Urgh,' said Violet.

'Your Tom would love this though,' she took out a tailcoat. 'Just like Fred Astaire's.'

'Check the pockets for clues,' said Violet, but they were empty, as were the two suitcases. They didn't even have name and address labels.

Gracie moved on to the lumpy mattresses, wondering if the Dixons had stashed any incriminating evidence beneath them, while Violet stuck her fingers into the pot plant's soil before wiping them clean on her trousers when her search proved fruitless.

'Nothing.' Gracie felt so disappointed. The Dixons were just a conjurer and an assistant. She felt a pang of guilt at having searched through the personal belongings of an innocent couple, but they had done it for the right reasons. 'We're no closer to finding Ma, and it's been hours, Violet.' She gulped, as the tears finally began to flow. 'I don't think we have any choice but to call the police.'

'Hey, come on. We're not giving up. The boys might've found something.'

Gracie tried to nod, but now her nose was running. 'Could you pass me a hanky,' she asked, pointing at the drawers where she'd seen one.

Violet rummaged for one. 'Here you are.'

Gracie shook open the cotton handkerchief and went to blow, but at the last moment she pulled the hanky away.

'Look,' Gracie passed the hanky to Violet. 'It's Ma's! See – she embroidered her initials on it – A. F. Annie Fairshaw.'

'Why would the Dixons have it? Does this prove they are responsible for your ma's disappearance?' said Violet.

Gracie wiped his eyes. 'It's a definite lead. Now I know we'll find Ma.'

'Definitely,' said Violet, passing the hanky back. 'We'd better tell the boys we've found a clue.'

Gracie reached out for the door and then froze.

The handle was already turning from the other side.

Chapter Seven
Phyllis Smells A Rat

'I knew I heard something!' It was Phyllis. 'What are you two up to?'

'You nearly gave me a heart attack,' said Gracie, shoving the hanky into her apron pocket.

'I nearly wet myself!' added Violet.

'Are those my keys?' Phyllis snatched them back. 'I've been looking everywhere for them.'

'We had to borrow them,' said Gracie. 'We thought we saw a rat go into the Dixons' room.'

'A RAT!' exclaimed Phyllis.

Gracie avoided Violet's eyes and tried to keep a straight face, 'but luckily it was only Fred.'

'Fred? Who on earth is Fred?' said the maid. 'You haven't got more friends in there, have you?'

'Fred's not a person,' said Gracie, giggling. 'He's George's pet rat.'

'A pet rat! In a boarding house – are you mad?' Phyllis seemed to soften. 'At least tell me you've caught it?' She stood on her tiptoes and peered over their shoulders. 'Good grief! Look at the state! I know you were planning to make some changes, but you really shouldn't reorganise rooms while guests are still staying in them.'

'Fred wasn't easy to find,' said Gracie, glancing back into the room. The bed sheets were all untucked and clothing was poking out of the chest of drawers and wardrobe doors. 'We might have made a bit of a mess.'

'A *bit*?' repeated Phyllis.

'Although, we did find him,' fibbed Violet, patting her dungarees pocket. 'Fred's safely tucked away,' she said with a squirm, 'but he's trying to get out again, so we should get going.'

'Hold your horses,' said Phyllis. 'You don't think you're leaving me to tidy up, do you? I might be a maid, but I'm not your servant. Why are the chamber pots in the middle of the floor? Tell me that rat's not had a wee in them?'

Gracie laughed. 'Rats don't use chamber pots, silly.'

'They wee and poo anywhere they like,' added Violet.

'Oh, you two are insufferable. Now get in there and put everything back as it was.'

Gracie and Violet watched as Phyllis stormed off with the keys, back towards the Fairshaw's private quarters.

'I can't believe we got away with it,' said Gracie, as they went back into the Dixons' room to tidy up.

'I know,' said Violet. 'Can't you smell the sweat?' she revealed her armpits. 'I was sure we were going to get caught.'

'When that door handle turned, I was terrified,' said Gracie. 'Still, it was worth the risk.'

***

The weather had taken a turn for the worse. Gracie was glad she'd thrown her coat on over her maid's outfit. The rain was coming down in bucketfuls and the air was icy cold.

Gracie and Violet ran to the shops where they found Tom and George shivering under the bus shelter.

'Told you we'd be finished first,' said Tom smugly, wrapping an arm around George's shoulder.

'Doesn't matter who was first, it matters who got a result,' said Violet.

'Ta dah!' Gracie showed them Ma's handkerchief. 'A clue. This is Ma's.'

'We found it hidden in the Dixons' chest of drawers,' Violet explained.

'So, we know they're responsible for Ma's disappearance,' added Gracie. 'Now we have to rescue her and make sure they are punished.'

'We can't do that on empty stomachs,' said Tom, 'George and I are starving.'

'We want to get some chips,' pleaded George.

Gracie checked her pocket for the shopping change. She scooped it into her palm. There was enough money for her and George, but she was too worried to eat.

'Oh, alright then, chips will warm you up. You look frozen,' she hugged her brother close.

Tom opened his arms and grinned at his sister.

'No chance,' said Violet.

***

Gracie was surprised when her belly rumbled as they all entered the chippy; she could smell the delicious aroma of golden fried potato. *I will have some, after all.*

The windows were all steamed up and George drew a funny face while they waited their turn. Gracie breathed in the salty, vinegary vapour. It was familiar and comforting. She felt better already.

At last their chips were dished up. Violet passed out the warm newspaper parcels and they walked back to the bus shelter.

They tore open the wrappings as they sat down.

'I'm so hungry, I could eat a donkey,' said George, shoving a fistful of chips into his mouth.

Gracie delved in with a finger and thumb and pulled out a fat, golden chip. She blew on it and bit the end off. There was something about sea air that made chips taste so good.

'This bad weather's here to stay,' said Tom, his mouth full of half-chewed spud.

He was right. There were more big black clouds gathering on the horizon.

'I hate getting rain on my chips,' said George, scowling. 'If I'd wanted them wet, I'd have ordered gravy like Violet.'

Violet laughed. 'Have a dip if you want.'

Tom waved a chip at her. 'Aww, thanks.'

'I didn't mean you,' but she still offered her tray in his direction.

'Ooh, lovely,' said Tom.

A seagull swept down and shook its wet wings, then hopped towards them. Gracie waved her arm at it and it hopped backwards. It stabbed at a squashed cold chip on the ground with its mustard coloured beak.

'It's injured,' said George. 'Look.'

The seagull had a misshapen webbed foot. Gracie steadied her parcel in the crook of her elbow and threw it a fresh chip.

The bird gave a happy squawk and hobbled after it.

'Hey, listen to this. This explains why Pa rushed out this morning,' said Violet, pointing at her newspaper wrapping.

'Who is Auntie Astra?' asked Gracie, peering closer.

'She writes the Blackpool Gazette's children's page,' Violet explained. 'Regular readers are invited to join a special club called The League of the Shining Star.'

So that was what Tom had been on about at the beach!

Tom read the article out.

Switch at the Switch-On

Dear League of the Shining Star,

The Mayor of Blackpool has asked the newly-crowned Railway Queen to do the honour of switching on the Illuminations this Saturday night.

The Mayor had been looking forward to performing the ceremony but has decided instead to hand over the task to fifteen-year-old Miss Elsie 'Audrey' Mosson, after meeting her this morning.

Alderman Whittaker said, 'Miss Mosson is a charming girl, with a frank and vivacious disposition – and I thought it would be very appropriate for this to be her first official duty as Queen.'

Many of you will be at the Switch-On tomorrow night and I am sure you will welcome Miss Mosson as we welcome all to Blackpool.

Love, Auntie Astra

Tom turned the paper around. They could see a cartoon drawing of Audrey at the top of the page.

'She looks like an ordinary teenager,' said Violet. 'Not a Queen.'

'She looks like Phyllis,' said George with a shrug.

The others stared at him.

'Blooming 'eck, he's right,' said Gracie, biting into another chip. The seagull gave another squawk and flew on to the roof of the chip shop.

'Who looks like me?'

Gracie span around. 'Phyllis! Will you please stop popping up like that? I nearly choked this time.'

'Let me see.' The maid reached out for the paper.

Violet tore off the sketch and handed it over.

'That Audrey sounds like a right little snob,' muttered Phyllis, 'waltzing round Blackpool in a tiara! I look nowt like her. Now, what are you lot *really* up to? What have you done with the other half of my keys – and don't give me anymore nonsense about Houdini-style escapee rodents.'

Gracie saw Violet suck in her lips tight. Tom folded his arms and George closed his eyes as though it would turn him invisible. She stood up straighter. 'If you want the truth, you have to promise not to tell another soul.'

Phyllis raised her eyebrow. 'Give me a chip while I think it over.'

Gracie offered her the bag.

'Thanks.' The maid picked out a plump chip. 'Now, what's the problem?' she asked between chews. 'I know something's going on.'

'It's our ma,' said Gracie. 'She's vanished.'

'What do you mean *vanished*?' asked Phyllis.

'She's been taken,' said Gracie, 'by the Dixons.'

'They're kidnappers,' added Violet. 'They've got Gracie and George's ma prisoner somewhere.'

'Don't be ridiculous. I've worked at The Majestic for a year – I would know if the Dixons were criminals.'

'It's true, listen . . .' Gracie recapped all that had happened.

***

'Are you sure the van driver called him Reginald Dixon? It might have been a joke, not an alias,' said Phyllis, taking the rest of her keys from Tom. 'Guests don't sign in with their first names, and I've never heard his wife call him Reg.'

'It *is* an alias,' insisted Violet, dropping her empty chip tray into the bin.

'He must have forced Ma into their room,' added Gracie.

'Mrs Fairshaw wasn't in there, though, was she?' said Phyllis, pulling a bemused face.

'No,' said Gracie, 'but her hanky was.' She took it out of her apron pocket to show her.

Phyllis inspected it. 'Well, that's hardly a smoking gun. They could have found it in the corridor. They're conjurers. I bet they've got thousands of handkerchiefs.'

'You're not listening,' said Gracie. 'One minute Ma was in our room, and the next – she was gone.'

'We found her hat and glasses.' said George.

'Her hanky too,' added Violet. 'In the Dixons' room.'

'Only, like Gracie said, they're not *really* called the Dixons,' added Tom.

'So, who *are* they really?' asked Phyllis, wrinkling her brow.

Gracie sighed.

'We don't know,' said Violet.

'We aren't making it up, honest Phyllis!' wailed George. 'Please believe us.'

'Hey, don't get all upset,' Phyllis continued. 'You've wound yourselves up proper, haven't you? Your ma has probably had to sort something out about the mortgage or other boring grown up stuff. She'll be back soon enough.'

Gracie looked at the others in frustration. Why wouldn't Phyllis believe them?

'Why don't you go and see a bit of Blackpool, before you go doolally with your imaginings. Miss Steele mentioned that the regulars are going to the Ballroom this afternoon. I bet you haven't even been in the Tower yet, have you? Don't worry about tea, I'll pick up some hot pies from the bakers later.'

Gracie sighed. 'Thank you, Phyllis.'

Now they knew where they would find the Dixons.

'You're welcome. Now finish your chips.'

Gracie watched as the maid headed back to The Majestic. 'Eat up, we're going to discover the Dixons' real names.'

Chapter Eight

A Stroke Of Luck

'If we're going to follow the Dixons around Blackpool, we'll need money for trams and taxis,' said Gracie. 'I've spent up.'

'We could go to the amusements arcade,' said Tom. 'There's a good one at South Pier. I've a couple of pennies left.'

'Aren't gambling machines set so that you always lose?' asked Gracie.

'I reckon I can work out how to make sure you win every time,' replied Violet.

Gracie wasn't convinced, but she didn't have a better idea.

They headed back to the top of Osborne Road, turning right in front of the Open Air Baths. There was still a light drizzle in the air.

'Raining again,' groaned George.

'It always rains for the Illuminations,' said Violet. 'It's as traditional as sideshows and sticks of rock!'

Huge white waves crashed on to the shrinking shore as the tide moved in.

They picked up speed, dodging around the A-boards advertising shows and other attractions.

The South Pier's glass pavilion entrance was book-ended by two scallop-roofed buildings.

'Blackpool has three piers,' said Violet, 'but this is my favourite, it looks like summat from a foreign country.'

'It is pretty,' agreed Gracie, 'but I wouldn't fancy cleaning all that glass!'

They passed through the entrance on to the pier deck. The damp wooden planks bounced slightly as they ran towards the arcade.

'Don't look down through the slats, George,' warned Gracie, 'you know it makes your legs go all wobbly.'

'Like jelly,' agreed George, looking a bit green.

The amusement machines were lined up like soldiers. Gracie studied the first machine. *I Tell Your Future* was emblazoned in gold across its front.

'What nonsense,' said Violet, pulling her away. 'Besides, we need to make money, not waste it.'

'This looks like a good machine,' said Tom. It was called *The Clock*. 'You put your penny in the hole, there at the top.'

He handed Gracie a coin and she placed it into the disc-shaped hole under the machine's name.

'Now you have to turn the handle – that makes the mechanism work,' said Violet.

Gracie followed the instructions and watched as the clock hands rotated.

'If the big hand stops on any of the hour numbers, you win that amount,' said Tom. 'But if you can get both hands to land on twelve, you get the big prize!'

The clock hands continued to turn. Gracie willed it to land on twelve o'clock. Would it ever stop?

The hands began to slow down as they approached the top of the clock face. 'It's nearly there!' she cried. But at the last moment, the hand twitched and flicked just past the winning spot.

'Ha, ha, ha, ha, ha!' called a seagull behind her.

Gracie glared at it. The seagull cocked its head to one side, then stretched out its neck and called again. 'Ha, ha, ha, ha, ha!' It waddled awkwardly towards her.

It was the seagull with the twisted foot again.

'Oh no,' said George. 'Better try again.'

'I'm not sure,' said Gracie. 'We've got even less money than what we started with now. I think these machines are made so you keep feeling like you're close to a win, when really – it's the arcade owner getting rich.'

'Hmm, that one might be fixed so it never pays out,' said Violet. 'Let's try another.'

Gracie shook her head, but as she did, the others moved deeper into the arcade.

'I reckon I'd be good at this one,' said George, gazing at a crane machine.

'We don't want sweets,' said Violet. 'We want hard cash.' She sighed.

'I think this was a bad idea,' said Gracie, quietly.

'Let's try one more,' said Violet. They did a circuit of the machines, dismissing a hen that laid egg prizes, a horse racing game and a fruit machine that looked very complicated.

'How about this one,' said Tom, pointing at wooden machine decorated with stars and flashes of light on a blue and metal panel. 'This one also takes real skill.'

'*Rockets,*' read George. 'I like the sound of that!'

'What do you think, Vi?' asked Tom.

'Seems straightforward, it's a bit like a pinball,' replied Violet, having read the wording on the front of the machine. 'The object of the game is to drop a ball into each of the three columns.'

'Let's have one last try,' said Tom, handing over another coin. Gracie thanked him and dropped it into the slot.

'Turn that star shaped knob slowly,' said Violet, 'it should release the first ball.'

Gracie twisted it to the left and a small silver ball moved into play position. Now she had to get it to fire upwards.

There was a pivoted lever in a cutaway space on the bottom right of the machine. She took a deep breath and sharply tapped the lever. A ball shot up and landed in the first column.

'Ha!' said Gracie. 'That was easier than I expected. One down, two to go.' She turned the knob again and a second silver ball was released.

'Want me to help?' asked George.

'No, thanks. Now, watch.' She put her fingers against the lever again and gave a blunt push. The ball soared and landed in the middle column.

The others clapped. Gracie noticed heads turning to see what was going on.

The man in charge walked over. 'You're doing well,' he said. 'You only need one more to win the jackpot. Still, the last one is always the hardest. Good luck though, lass.'

Gracie opened and closed her hand, loosening up the fingers. She turned the knob once more. The final silver ball glinted at her.

She placed her hand on the lever and gave a sharp tap. The ball fired up, up, up . . . but Gracie knew that it was too fast, too hard.

'Oh,' said George sadly, as the ball soared over the columns. 'Never mind.'

The silver ball fell to the bottom of the machine.

The man gave her a sympathetic smile, then strolled away.

'We should go,' said Gracie, but the ball had rolled back to the starting position. She hesitated. Did this mean she could have another go?

Gracie looked to Violet, who seemed to know what she was thinking. 'Try,' her new friend whispered, 'and whatever happens, I promise never to waste money on these silly machines again.'

Gracie adjusted her stance and placed her hand on the lever. She didn't really expect that it would move. Surely the game was over? She flicked the lever, and the ball flew up again.

Violet gave a surprised laugh. It was on target! Gracie stared in disbelief as the ball dropped firmly into the final column.

'Turn the handle,' said Tom, jumping up and down. 'Claim the jackpot!'

Gracie's hand felt sweaty as she wrapped her fingers around the star shape and twisted it. Her chest filled up with pride at the sound of cascading money.

Penny after penny poured out of the machine. The children gathered it all as quickly as they could, stuffing their trouser and coat pockets with the coins.

'We're rich!' cried Tom.

'Let's play again,' said George.

Gracie scowled.

'Oh no!' called the arcade owner. 'That's the second time this week – that machine must be faulty. I'm marking it out of order, now off you go!'

They ran away, giggling with delight as their winnings threatened to spill everywhere.

Chapter Nine

The Real Reginald Dixon

G racie and the others headed to the tram stop and joined the back of the queue. A double-decker cream and green tram was pulling into view.

'Great timing, it's the 252,' said Violet, checking her watch. 'She's one of the new trams. It will take around twelve minutes to get t' Tower – depending on how many passengers get on and off.'

'Thanks for the unnecessary information, Sis',' said Tom.

The tram was already packed, and Gracie wasn't sure there'd even be room for them. She wanted to wait for the next one, but Violet insisted they get on.

Gracie took a deep breath and stepped up and through the middle doors, clutching George's hand. It was standing room only downstairs. Violet pointed to the winding steps and they made their way to the upper deck.

It was busy upstairs too, but there was room towards the back. Gracie and Violet dropped down on to one of the wooden bench seats; Tom and George sat on the one behind.

The girls turned around so they could talk to them.

'I've been thinking,' said Gracie, 'if the Dixons are responsible for Ma's disappearance, knowing why they've taken her might help us work out where they have her hidden. If one of them is the guest Ma recognised from years ago, then why did they fall out? How did they know each other?'

'We need to find out more about the Dixons,' said Tom. 'Did they ever come to Milltown? Did your ma know just one or both of them?'

Gracie's stomach lurched as the tram moved off. She held on tight to the back of a seat and tried to focus on the view out of the window to take her mind off all the people crammed into a small space. A trickle of sweat rolled down the back of her neck.

After a couple of minutes, the tram stopped again. More passengers shuffled off and then more got on. Gracie gritted her teeth.

'You'll love the Golden Mile, George,' said Tom. 'There are loads of sideshows. They've got the World's Biggest Rat on display. Then there's a woman with a beard and a man with. . .'

'Oh no,' said Gracie. 'I think they're awful, those poor people being exhibited because they look different.'

'I quite agree,' said Violet, shooting her brother a look.

'Look, the Tower!' said Gracie, as the tram rattled along the prom. 'Not far now.'

***

They paid their entrance to the Tower, then sprinted through the foyer and up the stairs to the Ballroom.

The music hit as soon as you went through the doors. Loud, but not brash, the Wurlitzer's happy melody lifted Gracie's soul.

The ballroom was like a palace, with a beautiful painted ceiling and two rows of golden balconies.

The dance floor was heaving with couples swarming like waltzing bees. Gracie's heart began to race a little, but she stayed firmly on the carpet. She couldn't imagine anything worse than being squashed up in the thick of the dancers. Gracie could feel herself overheating, so she undid her coat.

'That's the *real* Reginald Dixon,' said Violet, pointing towards the stage and the man seated at the large white Wurlitzer organ. He ran his fingers over three layers of keys, adding the occasional flourish – his body swaying gently to the tempo. 'I'd love to take that Wurlitzer apart and see how it works.' She had to shout to be heard over the music and chatter.

'What about *our* Reginald Dixon?' said Gracie, leaning against a cool marble pillar. 'Can you see him yet?'

'You won't see owt hiding there,' said Tom. 'You need to dance!' He grabbed Gracie and swung her round.

Faces swirled around her.

'Stop it, stop it!' she cried, trying to pull free.

'Let her go,' said Violet. 'She doesn't like it.'

'Sorry,' said Tom, releasing her.

'She hates crowds,' explained George, as Gracie ran from the dance floor.

Gracie sank down on to a red velvet chair, breathing fast. 'I'll be fine in a minute,' she gasped. 'I just panicked. I didn't mean to shout, Tom.'

'I didn't mean to frighten you either,' he replied.

'Do you want to go outside, get some fresh air?' asked Violet.

'Thanks Violet, but I'll be alright in a moment. Besides, we came here to find the Dixons and that's what we're going to do.' Gracie reached into her apron pocket for Ma's handkerchief to mop her tears. It wasn't there. 'Oh no!' she cried. 'I've lost Ma's hanky!' She scanned the dance floor. *Had it dropped out there?* 'It could have fallen out anywhere between The Majestic and the Tower!'

'Don't worry, Gracie,' said George.

'We can still prove the Dixons are the kidnappers,' said Tom. 'You and George head t' balcony, you do one side and Violet the other.'

Gracie watched as he ran around the edge of the dance floor towards the stage. 'What is he doing?'

Tom turned and gave her a big grin, then gestured for her to go with a waft of his hand.

Gracie, George and Violet made their way to the curving staircase and jogged up the steps. They split up at the top. Gracie squeezed along the plush red seating on the right-hand side, Violet took the other and George stayed in the middle.

Gracie looked down on to the crowded dance floor, scouring it for dark-haired men and blonde women. A few times she thought she might have spotted the Dixons, but it was impossible to be certain.

The organist was lost in his performance, his fingers pressing the keys in a final flourish. Reginald Dixon swung around to address the audience. 'A modern quickstep next, for those of you feeling energetic . . .' he paused as Tom ran up the white steps on to the stage. 'Yes, son?'

Some of the dancers were returning to their seats. *Perhaps they prefer the slower pieces*, Gracie thought.

Tom was whispering into Reginald Dixon's ear.

What is he saying? Gracie wished she could hear, but only the organist could be heard on the microphone.

Suddenly, Reginald Dixon threw back his head and laughed. 'Ladies and gentlemen, boys and girls. If I could have your attention for one moment. It seems we have a very special guest here this evening.'

Violet raised her arms in a confused gesture.

'Yes, believe it or not – there are two of me! We have another Reginald Dixon in the ballroom tonight – this boy's father. Where are you, Mr Dixon?'

Everyone turned to look around for the other Reginald.

Gracie scoured the seating downstairs for anyone not swivelling around.

'There!' They all raced down the steps to the edge of the dance floor. The conjurer was sat with his wife and two other men at a table beside the dance floor. Both men had their backs turned to Gracie, but she could see one had red hair and was wearing a navy pinstriped suit – and the other – the silver chain of office. It had to be the Mayor of Blackpool.

Mr Dixon was playing it cool, but he was unnerved. He glared at Tom who was making his way to the gang from the stage, his eyes following him until they settled on Gracie. A scowl spread across the conjurer's face.

'You were brilliant,' said Gracie.

'If you think that's brilliant, you should see my quickstep,' said Tom.

'We should go,' said Gracie, feeling Mr Dixon's eyes still on her. So Reginald Dixon might be the mysterious guest's alias – but how could they prove it and find out the couple's real names?

'This one's for you, Reg!' and the organist burst into 'Well I Never'.

He can't do owt, thought Gracie, *not with the Mayor there.* She made her way back to George and Violet.

Suddenly, Tom was yanked back by a large hand. Gracie cried out – Mr Dixon had found them!

'What do you think you're playing at?' asked an angry male voice.

Gracie gasped – it was the red-haired man in the navy pinstriped suit from Dixon's table.

'Daddy!' squealed Violet.

Gracie breathed out in relief.

'We were just dancing,' said Tom.

Mr Emberton frowned. 'Not up there, you weren't. What was all that tomfoolery about?'

George giggled.

'You prancing about is one thing, but now you think you're a comedian! I suppose you were trying to impress her.' He narrowed his eyes at Gracie.

Violet hugged her pa hard. 'Never mind Tom, he's always being silly. What are you doing here? You hate dancing, Daddy.'

Mr Emberton cocked his head towards the Mayor. 'Last meeting with Alderman Whittaker. I thought everything was all ready for the Switch-On, but he wants to go over the details *again*. I'll be working until midnight at this rate.'

He does look tired, thought Gracie.

'Who is that with the Mayor?' asked Tom, casually. 'I'm sure I recognise him.'

'That's Peter Preston,' Mr Emberton replied. 'You know, Hey Presto!'

Gracie grinned. They now knew Mr Dixon's real name, and it had been unexpectedly easy to find it out!

Violet and Tom's pa was still talking. 'The Mayor wants to make this year's Illuminations the greatest yet,' continued Mr Emberton. 'It had better be – half of the transport budget is being spent on lights! No wonder they're splitting the Illuminations from the tram department.

'Peter will be performing his *Hey Presto!* magic show at the Switch-On ceremony. Did you not read my article about him in tonight's Gazette?'

The children shook their heads.

'It's a survival against the odds tale – proper rags to riches stuff!'

'We're so looking forward to the Switch-On ceremony, Daddy,' said Violet. 'I've been telling my new friend Gracie all about it. Do you think it would be possible for her and George to come as our guests?'

'That's not necessary,' said Gracie, she didn't want to sound rude, but there was no way she was going to the Switch-On. It would be heaving with people.

'Listen,' said Mr Emberton, distracted. 'I've got to get back to

Alderman Whittaker, and you pair should be heading home.' He flicked his wrist and tutted. 'I'm forever mislaying it.'

Violet blushed. 'Yes, we'd better see our friends to the tram stop, then we can get our bus.' She hid her father's watch behind her back and leaned in to kiss her pa's cheek.

'Don't wait up,' he said.

'We won't,' replied Tom.

***

Gracie and the others exited the Tower and strolled along the seafront to the tram stop. The temperature had really dropped, and the passing cars and trams had their lights on. They fastened up their coats to the top and huddled together on a wrought iron seat inside the shelter.

'So, Reginald Dixon's real name is Peter Preston,' said Gracie. 'Better known as Hey Presto, the conjurer.'

'The budgie tried to tell us,' said Violet. 'He kept saying "Hey Presto!", remember?'

'You're right,' said Gracie. 'I wonder why Presto uses a false name at The Majestic. It's not like he's that famous or owt. I've never even heard of Hey Presto!, have you?'

The others shook their heads.

'We should try to find out more about him,' continued Gracie. 'In less than twenty-four hours, Presto will have done his performance and he'll be packing up and moving on to another town for another show.'

We have to find Ma before the Switch-On or we might never find her, thought Gracie.

Tom pulled out an abandoned copy of the Gazette that had been shoved into the bin. He flicked through the pages while they waited.

'What exactly does your pa do?' asked Gracie.

'Pa works for the council – in the publicity department,' Violet explained. 'He helps advertise how brilliant Blackpool is. He has to think up catchy slogans. You know like *Blackpool – Progress* and *Blackpool: for healthy, happy holidays.*

'He has to organise the Switch-On an' all. Pa likes the details of each year's Illuminations to have an element of surprise. Last year they lit up the tower for the first time! This year they've booked Presto to perform.'

'And Pa writes for the Gazette,' said Tom, grinning at his sister. 'He covers all the big news stories about Blackpool, but he can't do it under his own name. Can you keep a secret?'

'Of course,' said Gracie.

George nodded.

'Pa writes the *League of the Shining Star* page,' said Violet, giggling. 'He's Auntie Astra!'

Gracie and George gasped.

'Ah, here's the article Pa mentioned,' said Tom. '*Peter Preston grew up in an orphanage, where he learned the skills that led to his career as a conjurer.*'

'You had to look out for yourself because no one else would,' Preston says. 'It began with me pocketing the odd bread roll from the kitchen; swiping it quickly so no one would see. Soon I learned to conceal all sorts up my sleeve – spoons, handkerchiefs, coins. After a while I was taking things for the challenge, not for the object itself.'

'Did your ma grow up in an orphanage, Gracie?' asked Violet, 'they might have met there.'

'No,' said Gracie. 'She was raised in Milltown, same as me and George.'

Tom read on. 'Unfortunately, one day I was caught trying to hide the orphanage's keys, so the master threw me out. I moved around a lot. Sold the few possessions I had acquired, took temporary jobs – and when they finished me – I pocketed what I needed to tide me over.'

'He sounds like a thief, not a conjurer!' said George.

'I agree,' said Gracie, crossly.

Tom continued. 'One day I saw a poster advertising a magic show. I scraped together enough money to buy a ticket. When I stepped into that hall, it was like stepping into another world. A place of colour and light.

'The conjurer wore a tuxedo and top hat and his voice was full of confidence. I knew in that moment that life was what I wanted more than anything. I went around to the stage door to say how much I'd enjoyed the show.

"This is your lucky day," he told me. "I need a new assistant."

'I was overjoyed. I learned how to make the brass rings connect and separate with a flick of my wrist, how to make coloured handkerchiefs appear at will and how to pull a rabbit out of a hat – but mainly I just packed and unpacked the conjurer's equipment and arranged his accommodation.

'The conjurer was older than me. He'd had every advantage in life, born into the right family and an education at the best college for young men.

'I realized I wanted what he had, and I was determined to have it all, and more . . .'

'Look!' Violet interrupted, pointing across the street.

Gracie turned to see Mr and Mrs Dixon – no, Preston – getting into a posh black car, with a badge depicting the Blackpool coat of arms on the bonnet. 'They're getting a lift from the Mayor,' she said.

'Don't worry, your tram's coming,' said Violet, pointing up the line.

'We'll see you in the morning,' said Tom, hugging her. 'We can help you with the breakfast.'

'Help burn it, more like,' said Violet.

Gracie chewed her lip. She hadn't even thought about the fact that she'd have to feed the guests again. *Oh, Ma*, she thought. *Where are you?*

Chapter Ten
Close Up Magic

There was a hubbub coming from the parlour as Gracie and George entered The Majestic.

'Hurry,' said Edna Hill, giddy with excitement.

'The show is about to start!' added Elspeth.

'Show?' asked Gracie. 'What show?'

Edna clapped her hands. 'You'll never believe it, but Mr Dixon is actually the conjurer Hey Presto! And he's going to do a special performance just for The Majestic!'

'We're getting a sneak preview,' added Elspeth. 'What a treat!'

The sisters ushered them inside.

'Presto insisted we wait for you and your brother to get back,' said Edna. 'He didn't want you to miss out.'

'Yes, he insisted on waiting for you to come home,' added Elspeth. 'Isn't he a lovely man?'

Gracie's nerves were on edge. Tom's ballroom trick had helped them find Presto's name, but now he knew they were following him.

'I'm hungry,' whispered George.

Gracie realised they hadn't had any tea. She wondered if there was any pie left. She beckoned Phyllis over.

'Did you have a nice time?' asked the maid.

'It was illuminating,' Gracie replied, 'but we forgot to eat anything.'

Phyllis shook her head. 'I'll fetch you a biscuit, but you must have something proper after the show.' Her face was suddenly serious. She glanced at the parlour clock. 'You know it is getting quite late and your ma's still not home. I must admit, I'm beginning to worry now. Maybe you were right all along, Gracie. What if she's had an accident or something? Perhaps I should ring the police and the hospital.'

'No,' said Gracie. 'I mean, not yet. I'll explain after the performance.'

Phyllis hesitated. 'All right. Go and sit down. I'll fetch those biscuits.'

A row of dining room chairs had been laid out facing into the room. A tablecloth decorated with stars had been draped over the parlour table. On top of that sat an array of illusions, playing cards, cups and a top hat.

Gracie and George sat next to Miss Steele. The Fishwick's boy was bouncing up and down in his chair. The Barker's little girl was swinging her legs in excitement.

The sound of a heavily-played piano filled the room and Gracie swung around. The Hill sisters were sharing the keys to create a fanfare. Presto entered the room wearing a tuxedo, flicking out the tails as he passed them.

There was a gentle applause as the sisters brought their accompaniment to an end.

Gracie was surprised to feel a sense of anticipation as Presto gave a bow. She was both curious and excited to see the conjurer's performance.

There was a firecracker flash and a huge puff of thick smoke. Mrs Preston had appeared! She wore a low-cut purple costume that showed off her long legs and her blonde hair was plaited across her head like a milk maid.

'Ooh,' went the audience.

The sisters played a little flourish on the piano. Mrs Preston wafted the smoke away, coughing hard. She stood to one side, swaying slightly.

She's drunk, realised Gracie.

The audience applauded enthusiastically. Gracie narrowed her eyes. If Presto could make his wife appear from nowhere, making Ma disappear would be just as easy.

Presto picked up the top hat and showed it to the audience, letting them see his fingers run around the brim – showing off the interior.

'Hey Presto!' Two long white ears appeared, and the conjurer pulled out a rabbit.

The audience called out 'bravo!' and clapped louder.

Phyllis snuck back in and passed a couple of digestive biscuits to Gracie and George. She sat down next to them.

Next came a trick where a rope was cut in two and then made whole again. Presto then held out a chain of gold rings and passed them to Miss Steele in the audience.

'Please can you show the audience that these are impossible to separate.'

Miss Steele studied the chain for some moments, pulling hard on each ring in turn. 'Yes, they won't come apart,' she agreed confidently.

'You mean, like this!' exclaimed Presto, suddenly throwing each ring individually into the air.

Mrs Preston stepped forward to catch them, but they slipped through her grasp and fell on to the floor.

Presto huffed and signalled to his wife to fetch his next illusion. She stumbled, colliding with a smaller table and knocking several marked playing cards on to the floor. He grunted and shoved her out of the way, then picked up a large empty bird cage and brought it to the front.

Presto pulled out a silk scarf from out of his sleeve and wafted it over the cage, letting it billow like a sail until a yellow budgie was revealed.

'Here we have an ordinary budgerigar,' said Presto. 'Shall I turn Sunny into a beautiful parrot?'

'Oh yes,' called the sisters, thrilled at the idea, as a cloud of scarlet feathers exploded above the cage.

'Or a flamingo perhaps?' suggested Presto. This time there was a flash. An explosion of pink feathers burst from nowhere above the budgie.

The sisters snorted with laughter. 'Imagine!'

'I know . . .' He wafted the scarf over the cage again. 'The perfect choice for Blackpool.'

'Ha ha ha ha ha ha!' called a voice from under the material.

With a final flutter, the scarf vanished – revealing a grey seagull.

The audience burst into laughter.

The bird was standing awkwardly. Gracie realized that it was the seagull from earlier; her breathing rising as anger filled her chest.

Presto must have caught it.

The conjurer passed the cage to his wife, who put it down at the back of the room. The seagull was clearly distressed, pecking at the bars in frustration.

Gracie stood up. 'It's a wild creature. It shouldn't be trapped inside a cage.'

The other guests began to murmur. She wasn't sure if they

agreed with her or not, but she didn't care. She'd had enough of Presto and his cruelty.

Gracie marched across to the cage and picked it up. 'I'm letting this bird go.'

'Hurrah!' George cheered.

Presto just laughed and carried on with his performance.

Gracie pushed past Mrs Preston. 'It's deformed,' the assistant slurred. 'It won't survive on its own. It would be kinder to put it out of its misery.'

Bile rose in Gracie's throat, but she swallowed it back down. She would not let her see how upset she was.

She carried the seagull out of the parlour; the sound of Presto's voice fading away. There was nothing magical about his show. It was just a series of tricks and deceptions.

She put down the cage so she could open the door. The coolness of the night helped her to recover her composure. Minding her fingers, Gracie undid the clasp on the roof of the cage.

The seagull gave a loud cry and clumsily hopped out. The bird spread its wings and began to run awkwardly along the pavement. It pushed its webbed feet hard against the ground to launch itself, flapping its wings for extra thrust – and finally, it was airborne.

Gracie felt her heart leap as the seagull soared high above her head. It was finally free.

Chapter Eleven

Find The Lady

'Well done,' whispered Phyllis, as Gracie returned to her seat. Meanwhile, Presto was starting a new trick. He reached under the table and pulled out three blue and white teacups, then laid them upside down in a row. 'I have three identical cups.'

'Ooh, they are just like ours,' said the Hill sisters, taking their teacups off the top of the piano and waving them in the air.

Presto lifted each cup in turn to show the audience. 'Nothing inside them,' he wafted his hand over the top, 'and nothing above. Just ordinary teacups.'

'This game is called *Find the Lady*,' said the conjurer. 'This is the Lady,' he held a ping-pong ball between his thumb and finger, flicked it into the air and then caught it in a cup.

'I place the Lady under one of the cups.' He hid the ball under the middle one. 'Then we switch the cups around.' He put his hand on the cups bases and skated them around. Left over right. Middle over left. Always keeping them tight to the table.

He moved precisely. Gracie was able to follow the cup containing the Lady with ease.

Presto came to a stop. 'Where is the Lady?' he asked, wriggling an eyebrow.

'The left one!' called the audience pointing to the cup, but Gracie knew the Lady wouldn't be there.

'Are you certain?' he asked.

'Yes!' called the audience.

'Would you stake money on it?' asked Presto.

Mrs Preston staggered forward with a large glass jar half-filled with coins. The label on the front read: *FOOLS' GOLD*.

Everyone laughed.

Gracie didn't find it funny; she was sure Presto normally tricked people out of their money. She was pretty sure he'd pinched those teacups from the Hill sisters' room too.

Suddenly, the jar was flying through the air. Mrs Preston had slipped and now the money was clattering on to the floor. 'Sorry, sorry,' she mumbled, trying to scoop up the coins.

'Leave it, leave it,' growled Presto.

The conjurer straightened his back and took a deep breath. He lifted the end cup.

Everyone gasped. The Lady was not there.

'The right one,' shouted Elspeth and Edna.

Presto lifted the cup. Still no Lady.

'It must be the middle one,' said Miss Steele, confidently.

The conjurer turned it over. There was no Lady.

'Sisters, would you please show everyone your teacup again . . .'

They giggled and reached out for their cups. 'It's here!' they cried. 'We've found the Lady!'

All of a sudden, the lights went out – turning the room black.

'Of all the moments . . .' moaned one of the sisters in the darkness.

'Ow!' wailed Mrs Preston, 'stupid table.' She must have banged into it.

'Everybody stay where you are,' said Miss Steele. 'It's just a power cut. This weather will be to blame.'

'I'll check the fuses,' called Phyllis.

Gracie tapped her foot anxiously. *Was this Presto's doing?*

***

'What is taking so long?' grumbled the Hill sisters as the minutes passed by.

The longer the lights were off, the more concerned Gracie became that Presto had done it to buy time – as a distraction.

'George,' she whispered, 'you know all those things Ma says you're not allowed to have?'

'Yes,' he replied cautiously, 'you mean, like my pen knife?'

'Yes, as well as your catapult and the box you keep spiders in. Do you still have them, George?'

'I might have.'

'What about matches?' asked Gracie. 'Might you have some of them?'

There was some kind of kerfuffle going on behind them. It sounded like the Hill sisters were trying to make their way to the window.

'Where is it?' asked Mr Fishwick. 'It must be here somewhere.'

George rustled in his pocket. 'Only a couple, in case we need to make a campfire or signal for help. You know, if we get shipwrecked.'

Gracie tightened her hand around the packet of matches. She pushed back the envelope cover with her thumb. Only two remained.

'Helen, my watch must have dropped on to the floor,' continued Mr Fishwick. 'I think Benjamin's been fiddling with it again. Benjamin, have you got Daddy's watch?'

The sisters had pulled open the curtains at last. Gracie grabbed a candlestick from the mantelpiece.

She was relieved to see Presto and his wife were still in the parlour.

She passed the envelope to her brother. 'Light the candle, please.'

George's eyes widened. He struck the match and held it to the wick.

'I'm going to help Phyllis,' said Gracie.

'Are you sure you can manage it with, well . . . you know?' asked Elspeth.

'Yes. Wouldn't it be better if I went to check the power? Electricity can be dangerous,' said Presto. 'We wouldn't want you to have an accident.'

'I'll be fine,' replied Gracie, hoping that wasn't a veiled threat. 'I've always found ways to do what needs to be done.' She kept her voice steady, though her heart was racing.

The main light flickered back to life and the room was lit up again. Mr Fishwick was on his hands and knees looking under the chairs. 'It's very expensive. It was a present.'

Presto leaned forward and blew out Gracie's candle. 'Very able, aren't you? You wouldn't think it to look at you. I suppose you take after your mother.' He reached out a hand as though to tuck her hair behind her ear. A gold watch glinted on his wrist. She was sure it hadn't been there during the performance.

'It's not a family trait, it comes from being a Milltowner,' said Miss Steele, taking the candlestick.

Gracie flinched, as he drew back his hand. 'Well, where did that come from?' he held open his palm, revealing a green button. It was the one from Ma's coat.

Gracie felt faint with fear.

'Show's over, everyone,' Phyllis was back. Gracie felt a sense of relief flood over her.

'I think we should head to our beds in case the electricity goes off again,' said Miss Steele. 'Do you need any help putting your props away?'

Gracie rushed towards the maid, her hand clamped around Ma's button. She wanted to get as far away from the Prestons as possible.

***

'Here we go,' said Phyllis, putting two plates on the table. 'Eat up now.'

Gracie had updated the maid on everything that happened since they'd seen her outside the chippy, including the fact she was certain Presto had just stolen Mr Fishwick's watch.

'What if he does something like that at the Switch-On?' asked Gracie. 'What if he turns off the Illuminations and tries to steal something really valuable?'

'Like what, Blackpool Tower?' laughed Phyllis.

'I don't know, there'll be lots of important people on that platform, won't there? Dignitaries and VIPs – they're bound to have nice watches and bracelets and things.'

'You need to eat something,' said Phyllis. 'You're going to make yourself poorly. Your ma wouldn't like seeing you fading away.'

'I only missed one meal,' said Gracie, crossly, 'and I'm having it now, aren't I?'

George piled a large helping of mashed pie on to a piece of bread and butter. 'I love pie butties, don't you?' he said, sinking his teeth in. 'Can I give my crusts to Fred?'

'Ah, the famous Fred,' said Phyllis, forcing a smile. 'Go and get him then.'

Gracie stared at her supper, feeling queasy at the rich, meaty smell, but she forced a small amount of pastry into her mouth. It was like chewing cardboard.

'Where is Ma, Phyllis?' said George with a yawn, returning with his pet rat.

Phyllis busied herself at the sink. Gracie wasn't sure if she was avoiding Fred or the truth. 'She'll be home tomorrow; Gracie and I will make sure of it. Now, if I remember correctly, there's an old cage in the shed that belonged to Mrs Yates's son – he had a gerbil or a hamster. I can look for it in the morning, if you like?'

'Oh, yes please,' said George.

'It's time for your bed now, George,' said Gracie. 'Would you like to sleep in Ma's bed tonight?'

He nodded.

Gracie and Phyllis walked with him to Ma's bedroom and tucked him in.

SLAM!

'What was that?' asked George.

'The front door,' said Gracie.

'Go check,' said Phyllis, 'I'll stay with your brother.'

Gracie checked her key around her neck and crept down the corridor. She pulled back the lock and eased open the front door.

She peered out into the lamp-lit street. The cold air was like a slap to the face. She hesitated, wondering if she should go back for her coat, but then she might never catch up with whoever it was.

Gracie gritted her teeth and stepped out of The Majestic, pulling the door behind her. She could make out a figure weaving in and out, making their way along Osborne Road towards the seafront.

She hurried past the other houses and the parade of shops. The street seemed very different at night – grey and unwelcoming. Gracie picked up her speed as the figure seemed to slow. She realised then that they were dragging a suitcase.

One of the guests was leaving.

***

'Wait!' called Gracie. 'Don't go.' Her voice echoed too loud in the quiet street, but she didn't care.

The person stalled . . . and slowly turned.

Gracie ran, the cold air tight in her chest. As she got closer, the person's features came into focus.

A woman.

It was Mrs Preston.

Her eyes were red; mascara had run down her face.

'Did he send you after me?' asked Mrs Preston, her eyes unreadable. *Hopeful? Surprised?* Gracie supposed years of being a conjurer's assistant had taught her to mask her emotions.

'Are you leaving?' asked Gracie. A silly question, she could kick herself. 'Where are you going, Mrs Preston?'

'What do you care?!' She let go of her suitcase and it toppled over with a heavy thud. She slumped down on to it. 'Where's that stupid taxi?'

Gracie shivered. She should go back, there was no point trying to have a conversation with someone who'd clearly had a bellyful of drink.

'My husband doesn't want me anymore,' said Mrs Preston quietly.

Gracie sighed. 'I'm sure that's not true.'

''Tis,' slurred Mrs Preston. She was shaking her head, lost in her distress, but then slowly her eyes began to focus on Gracie. 'You!' she spat, jumping up. 'Haven't you caused me enough heartache?' There was a manic, hateful look in Mrs Preston's eyes.

'I don't know what you mean,' said Gracie, frightened. She tried to keep her voice steady and calm, so she wouldn't provoke her.

'Miss Goody two shoes, Little Miss Perfect,' sneered Mrs Preston, jabbing a finger at Gracie. 'I could never measure up to you.' She kicked the suitcase. 'I could never compare. Annie flaming Fairshaw.'

Gracie gasped. Mrs Preston had mistaken her for Ma. She probably did look like a younger version of her mother – *but how would Mrs Preston know that?*

'What do you know about my Ma? Where is she?' Gracie grabbed at Mrs Preston's coat collar.

'She's back,' said Mrs Preston, clasping a hand to her face, 'and now he doesn't need me. Doesn't want me . . .'

'You're not making much sense,' said Gracie. Did she mean Ma was back at The Majestic? She rubbed her arm to warm it up and tried to back away.

'I tried, I really tried,' wept Mrs Preston, fiddling with a gold chain around her neck. 'I should never have trusted a conman conjurer; I should have known he was conning me too! I was merely your replacement; an understudy stepping in until the day you returned.'

It dawned on Gracie. *Ma was Presto's first assistant!*

'He said you could read his mind,' continued Mrs Preston. 'You would distract the audience with a look or a movement, and then Peter would make the switch or palm an object. I can never guess what he's thinking, not on stage, not in our real life. Now he's kicked me out of the act – and out of our marriage. All I'm left with is a few silly baubles,' she pulled at the chain around her neck, flashing a blue sapphire pendant at Gracie.

Mrs Preston staggered to her feet. A taxi was coming toward them. The driver pulled into the kerb.

Gracie walked back to The Majestic. Her head was spinning with a series of images flashing in her mind. Ma dressed in a short, glitzy costume. Ma next to the conjurer, climbing willingly into the conjurer's cabinet. How could Ma have worked with a man like Presto?

Chapter Twelve

The Conjurer's Assistant

racie leaned against the boarding house's front door; delaying entering by turning her key over and over in her hand.

Ma had been missing for twelve hours. She would never have left her and George alone willingly. Gracie knew as soon as she got back to The Majestic, she would have to ask Phyllis to come with her to the police station in the morning.

So, Peter Preston was a conman. A trickster. But did that mean Ma had helped him too? Gracie didn't want to believe Mrs Preston, yet she could barely bring herself to tell Phyllis what she'd said. So how on earth would she be able to tell the police?

***

'So, who was it?' asked Phyllis, as soon as Gracie opened the door to the Fairshaw's rooms. 'Gosh, you look frozen. Come on and get warm by the fire, I'll pour you a hot cocoa.'

Gracie followed her to the kitchen and pulled a chair closer to the heat.

Phyllis put a pan of milk on to warm and scooped the cocoa powder into a cup.

'It was Mrs Preston, she's packed up and gone.'

'No!' gasped Phyllis. 'Did you speak to her, then?'

Gracie nodded and retold their encounter. 'I think she was telling the truth about Ma being his assistant and about him being a conman, but I don't want to believe that Ma helped him trick people.'

'Of course you don't. So – let's look at this logically. I'm going to give you some scenarios. Right, what would your Ma do if she found a purse in the street?'

'She'd hand it in at a police station,' replied Gracie, certain of this.

'What if a shopkeeper gave her too much change?'

'She'd tell them straight away,' replied Gracie, smiling.

'Exactly, as any honest person would. You're a good judge of character, Gracie Fairshaw. You were right about the Prestons and I know you're right about your Ma. Now, speaking of police stations, I'm going down there first thing, in case Presto tries to do a flit like his wife.'

'I think I might know where there's more evidence,' said Gracie. 'I noticed Mrs Preston was wearing a sapphire necklace and I'm sure it's is the one Edna Hill lost yesterday. I wrote a description of it in the lost property book and I noticed that quite a lot of things have gone missing at The Majestic.'

'I suppose there *has* been a few things over the years, but I don't think that's unusual. We can check properly in the morning. You need to get some sleep, Gracie.' Phyllis stirred the warm milk and poured it into the cup. 'Drink this and I'll fetch your nightie. Then you can get in with George.'

'Could you stay tonight?' asked Gracie. 'I'll let you have my bed.'

Phyllis smiled. 'If it would make you feel better.'

***

Though exhausted, Gracie slept badly, and she was relieved to be awoken by Phyllis coming into Ma's room with tea and toast.

'Did you hear that thunder last night?' asked Phyllis. 'It was like cymbals! Kept waking me up.'

'I don't remember, maybe. I didn't sleep well either. I had an awful nightmare. I was looking all over The Majestic for Ma. Then I found this magic cabinet with Ma's face on it. The next thing, I was trapped inside it and I could hear Presto sawing through the wood!' She shuddered.

'How awful! Well, don't worry, as soon as I've done the

breakfast, we'll go down to the police station. We don't want the guests – especially Peter Preston – knowing anything is up.'

Gracie gently woke George and they both sat up to eat.

Afterwards, they went to their rooms to get dressed. Gracie looked at her maid's outfit and decided she wanted to wear something more practical. She picked out a pair of dark blue trousers, which were more suitable than a skirt for the cold and wind – especially if they were going to be out late again. Even George had agreed to wear full length trousers. It may be September, but the weather didn't seem to realise. It had been chucking it down all morning, so they'd pulled on woollen jumpers and socks too, before adding their thick coats and hats.

Gracie nipped out into the corridor and collected the guest signing-in book and the lost property book. She laid them open on the kitchen table, her mouth watering at the smell of fried sausages and eggs.

'George, will you help me please?'

He nodded, wiping his greasy lips. 'What do I have to do?'

'I need you to read out any dates when the Prestons were staying at The Majestic.'

'Read?' he sighed. 'I thought you wanted me to wear a disguise and follow the Prestons!'

'I promise if there's any dressing up to do, I'll ask you, but for now I want to compare the dates against the lost property book.'

In among the lost umbrellas, walking sticks, forgotten gloves and scarves and mislaid glasses and pipes, were a few more valuable items. The odd purse, compact mirror, pocket watch, cigarette case and items of jewellery. On most occasions, the missing item coincided with a visit from the Prestons.

'How did Mrs Yates not notice the pattern?' asked Phyllis, as she dished up the breakfast.

'The Prestons altered the times of their visits. May, August, September, even Christmas, but always when The Majestic was at its busiest,' Gracie explained. 'They even reported their own items missing to cover their tracks. See, here . . . Mrs Preston reported she had lost a pair of gold earrings.'

'That's really sneaky,' said George.

'Well, they are tricksters,' said Gracie, opening the door to the dining room. 'Their career has been built on misleading people. They never stored their magical equipment here before, so Mrs Yates wouldn't have realised they were a conjuring act, or that they were using a false name.'

'Well I never,' said Phyllis, getting out the ingredients for making jelly and custard.

Gracie stood in the kitchen doorway, waiting for Presto to come in, while the last few Majestic guests received their breakfasts. The plates had barely touched the tablecloth before the breakfasts were devoured, as if it was a race to see who would finish first.

Tom and Violet came over to The Majestic at 8 a.m. They were also dressed for cold weather. Tom had on a flat cap and a tartan scarf, while Violet wore a woolly hat and her auburn hair in two plaits finished with ribbons. Gracie told them all about the conjuring show, Mrs Preston's disappearance and the missing valuables.

'The Prestons have been stealing belongings for some time. The matching dates are too much of a coincidence,' said Gracie. 'I'm also convinced they use their conjuring act as a distraction when they want to take more valuables.'

'We're going to take the books to the police station,' said Phyllis. 'They'll want them for evidence.'

They decided to play a game of Snakes and Ladders to pass the time until the end of breakfast, George insisted on rolling the dice for everyone.

Solving the mystery of Ma's disappearance felt a bit like the game they were playing. One minute you were making progress, the next you were back at the beginning.

'Do you think Presto intends to replace Mrs Preston with your Ma?' asked Tom, after they'd heard the revelation about Annie Fairshaw's past.

'You can't force someone to work for you, or to love you for that matter,' said Violet. 'He'll have to let her go or . . .' she clammed up.

'What if Ma has gone with him willingly?' asked Gracie, quietly.

'That's nonsense,' said Violet. 'This Presto fella takes what he wants; he's a conman. There will be a perfectly reasonable explanation as to how your Ma knows him. I wouldn't believe a word his bitter wife said.'

'A six!' called George, moving his counter up the ladder.

'Presto must be holding her against her wishes,' Violet assured Gracie.

'Probably got her locked up in one of his cabinets,' said Tom quietly. 'That one with the lady painted on it.'

'No,' said Gracie, 'we already checked that cabinet and it was empty.'

'We could double check it,' said Violet. 'The cabinet is still in his room; he must be saving it for his big performance.'

'We can't do that until he comes down for breakfast,' said George, rolling the dice again.

The front doorbell rang.

'Who could that be?' asked Gracie. 'I'd best answer it.'

She exited the Fairshaw's private quarters and hurried down the guest corridor to the front door.

Gracie opened it. 'Oh!'

It was a constable.

'May I come in?' he asked, taking off his helmet.

'Yes, of course.' She showed him into the parlour, her heart thudding. 'Has something happened? Has there been an accident?'

Had they found Ma?

'Are you Miss Fairshaw?' he asked, his face serious. He leaned on the fireplace mantel and took out his notebook and pencil.

'Yes, I am.' She swallowed hard.

'You are the young woman,' the constable hesitated, 'girl, that telephoned the station this morning?' He scribbled something down in the notebook.

Gracie shook her head. 'We don't have a telephone, although I was going to come to the station after breakfast...'

The constable wasn't listening. He straightened his back and wagged his finger. 'Prank telephone calls are a very serious matter, Miss. It's lucky for you that I answered the call and not the desk sergeant. We are extremely busy down at the police station preparing for tonight's Switch-On. We don't take kindly to time-wasters.'

'Time-wasters?' asked Gracie. 'I don't understand, Constable.'

The constable narrowed his eyes. 'Do you deny asking to speak to a detective? That you wanted them to investigate a conjurer for making a lady vanish?' He peered down his nose at her. His eyes were steely grey.

'I didn't make that telephone call... I mean, I was going to ...' Gracie shook her head in confusion. She took a deep breath. 'Constable, I was going to report a missing person. And there is a conjurer staying here at The Majestic, and I do think he has something to do with it.'

'If this is a silly prank . . .'

'I promise, it isn't, Constable. Please, you've got to help.'

'Hmm. Well, I suppose there's no harm in questioning this man. As you say, a missing person case is an important matter. Do you have any missing guests?' the constable poised his pencil over his notebook.

'No,' said Gracie, 'all our guests are accounted for. We only have a small number staying with us. Shall I escort you to room number three?'

The constable nodded. He snapped his notebook shut and put it back into his chest pocket.

Gracie led the way to Presto's room and knocked on the door. After a few seconds, the conjurer answered. He looked startled at seeing the constable.

'Is there a problem?' asked Presto. He was holding a white rabbit in his arms.

'If I could come inside,' said the constable.

'Of course.' He seemed to struggle with the animal for a minute. Presto and the constable both tried to step aside for each other, bumping together.

'Sorry, Constable. I was just gathering my belongings together.' He stepped backwards and placed the rabbit into his top hat. 'I check out this morning.'

Gracie peered into the room. The conjurer's cabinet had been dragged into the centre of the room, with all its doors wide open. It was still empty.

'You're a conjurer,' said the constable, reaching fruitlessly into his pocket for his notebook

'Yes,' said Presto. 'I was staying here incognito, but it seems my secret is out,' he smiled at Gracie. 'A conjurer must protect his secrets. If the audience knows how an illusion is done, it spoils the magic.' He put the top hat on to his head.

The constable laughed. 'The rabbit?' he asked, patting his other pockets.

Presto put a finger to his lips. The constable glanced around the room.

'Have you lost something?' asked Presto.

'We have had a report of a vanished lady.'

'Ah,' the conjurer raised an eyebrow at Gracie. 'That will be my wife – we came to a mutual decision that we should break up the act and our marriage. I can assure you she is fine, she has gone back to her mother.'

'Sorry to hear that, sir,' said the constable. 'Do you mind if I have a quick look around?'

'Of course not,' replied Presto, 'be my guest.'

Gracie watched as the constable made a cursory inspection of the room. 'Shouldn't you check the cabinet?' she interjected. She looked around. Something was telling her she was missing an important clue.

The constable gave a snort, then stood inside the cabinet,

hammering on the walls and ceiling.

'Want me to lock you in?' asked Presto.

'That won't be necessary, I can see it's a perfectly ordinary box,' replied the constable, spotting his notebook on the floor. 'Well, that's me done.' He picked it up and put it safely into his pocket. 'I'll write up my report, but I don't see any reason to trouble you any further. I would like another word with you though, Miss.'

Gracie led the constable back to the front door.

He paused at the threshold. 'Let this be a warning to you. If I find out you've made any more prank phone calls, I'll have you thrown in a police cell.'

'But he's lying, the missing person is my ma not his wife.' Gracie bit her tongue. There was no point trying to convince him. He wasn't going to give her a fair hearing. She forced out a few words of contrite thanks, though she was burning with anger.

He put his helmet back on. Job done.

Gracie let him out. She watched the constable walk back towards the promenade and noticed a familiar van driving down Osborne Road.

The *Tower Removals* van pulled up in front of The Majestic. She watched as the driver and his mate got out and approached the boarding house.

'I can't believe we've got to shift this lot again,' said

the driver.

Gracie tried to calm herself. If the police wouldn't help, then she would carry on investigating herself.

'Please, follow me.' She led them inside. 'I must say we'll be glad to have all that magic apparatus taken away. Our guests have been complaining about the doves cooing. White rabbits and the like belong in a magic shop not a boarding house.'

'Oh, we're not going to The Abracadabra,' said the mate.

'Aren't you? Where is it going then? Not the Imperial Hotel?' she joked.

'Almost! We've got to take it to the Town Hall,' said the driver. 'They want it all in place for the run-through at four o'clock.'

Gracie smiled at having gained new information. 'You know where to go? Room Three,' she tucked herself behind the reception nook and pretended to be busy with some letters. She wanted to see Presto leave.

The men removed the cabinet first, it made a right racket as they dragged it along the floor. Then they returned for Presto's suitcase, his tricks and, of course, his animals.

Finally, Presto came out. He strolled up to the reception nook and placed several bank notes on to the counter.

Gracie counted them, half expecting them to turn into useless coloured pieces of paper as she did so. 'Your key, please,' she added, her chest tightening.

He clapped his hands together and opened them to reveal his key.

Gracie took it and hung it up on the wall.

She watched him leave, then unhooked the key and crept back to his room.

***

Gracie let herself into number three. The room looked different now it was empty. It was just an ordinary bedroom again.

She hesitated and stared round the room. Something was different.

Her breath was rapid. She studied the room, trying to figure out what had changed.

At last – she worked out what it was. It was so big that she had overlooked it at first.

A door.

She was certain it hadn't been there when she and Violet had searched the room.

How could a door suddenly appear?

She stared at it, trying to picture the old layout of the room.

The wardrobe! Presto had sneakily dragged it in front of the adjoining door.

Gracie could see it all now. Ma returning to her room, Peter turning up, the two of them having some casual conversation at first. Then when he'd pushed for her to consider coming back to the act – to him – Ma must have said no.

While his wife was being sick in the communal toilet, he must have forced Ma into his room and then into the adjoining one – because this floor was just like the one above. The Hill sisters had adjoining rooms – and this room adjoined with its neighbouring empty one.

He had probably gagged and tied her, forced her into that room's wardrobe and then locked the door, concealing it by dragging the wardrobe from their room in front of it. Then later, he had transferred her into the conjurer's cabinet. She was sure of it.

But how had he smuggled Ma out of The Majestic if she was no longer in the cabinet?

Gracie's tears burned hot as she thumped the mattress hard with her fist.

***

After a few minutes, Gracie got up and went to find George and the others. She had to get out of the boarding house to think clearly. She was not going to let Peter Preston win. She was going to find Ma, rescue her and make everyone see the truth about Presto.

Phyllis and the others were doing the dishes.

'Who was at the door?' asked George.

'A constable,' Gracie replied, starting to put the dry crockery away.

'Oh, that is good news. Well, you can stop worrying now, the police will find your ma. Now, why don't you all head down to the beach?' said Phyllis. 'I'll make you up a little picnic. Something sweet will be best.' She started to rummage in the larder.

***

Half an hour later, Gracie and the others slumped into a row of deckchairs at the South Shore. They pulled their thick coats around them as they sheltered against the sea wall.

Gracie passed around jam butties and a flask filled with strong, sweet tea. The strawberry and soft white bread made a perfect combination, even when the odd grain of sand blew into her mouth.

'George, why don't you look for seashells while I chat to Violet and Tom?' suggested Gracie, wiping the last of the jam from her lips.

'Leaving me out again,' he tutted. 'I am old enough to . . . look at that crab!' he cried suddenly, dashing across the sand.

'You all right now, Gracie?' asked Violet.

She nodded slowly; too afraid she would blurt everything out if she tried to speak.

'Got it!' sang George, running towards them with the crab. 'It's a smasher, isn't it, Tom?' He let it dangle, its legs wriggling. 'I reckon we should put it in Presto's bed!'

Violet giggled. 'It's a nice idea, but what has the crab done to deserve such a fate?'

George laughed. 'I'll put it back then. I've got a better idea.'

Gracie watched as he started stuffing his coat pockets with slimy seaweed. 'It's too late, any road,' she said. 'Presto's gone.'

'What do you mean, gone?' asked Tom.

'Cleared out. Scarpered. Bolted,' said Gracie. 'He checked out.' She told them all about the constable, his search – and the empty conjurer's cabinet.

'Well, he can't have gone far,' said Violet. 'He's performing at the Switch-On tonight.'

'After last night's rehearsal, I'm convinced he's planning a big con tonight,' said Gracie. 'I think he will sabotage the Lights, so he can steal something valuable. I'm worried that he'll force Ma to assist him.'

'So, we think of a way to foil his plans,' said Tom. 'We need to set a trap.'

'A trap?' said George, overhearing on his return. 'We could dig a hole and fill it with snakes from the Tower menagerie. Then we can cover it with sticks and leaves. When Presto stands on it – CRASH! – he falls in.'

'Not that kind of trap,' said Gracie, trying not to laugh.

***

They discussed ideas as they walked through the drizzle to Osborne Road, but the suggestions were either too elaborate or unreliable.

They traipsed into The Majestic and through to the back. They took off their wet coats and hung them up on the hat stand to dry before finding Phyllis in the kitchen.

The maid was lifting a large cage on to the table. 'I found it, George. Go and fetch Fred.'

George dashed to his room and returned with his pet rat.

'He really is quite cute, isn't he,' said Phyllis, admiring the white rodent.

'The cage needs some paper to line the bottom,' said George.

'Try the parlour,' suggested Phyllis. 'Mr Barker usually leaves his copy of the Gazette in there.'

George went to find it.

'You should see what my brother did to his suitcase,' said Gracie. 'He made holes in it, so Fred could breathe!'

'Well, that is practical,' said Violet. 'Otherwise Fred might have suffocated.'

George was soon back with the Gazette.

The maid laid the newspaper out on the table.

George leaned over. 'I still think you look like the Queen, Phyllis,' he said, staring at the top page.

'What are you on about?' asked Phyllis.

'Miss Audrey Mosson,' he said in a pretend posh voice, showing them a photo of the Railway Queen. 'You could pretend to be her and run off with her tiara!'

'I'd quite like a tiara,' said Phyllis, 'and it would be a hoot pressing the Switch-On button in front of all those folk.'

'A tiara?' said Gracie. 'I bet that's what Presto is after! But how do we stop him?'

'We could put handcuffs on him,' said George.

'He's a conjurer, they can get out of any lock,' said Phyllis. She crossed her wrists and mimed breaking out.

'We need to work out how he's planning to steal the tiara. Violet, Tom, how much do you know about the plans for the Switch-On ceremony?'

'Bits,' said Tom. 'I know the button is pressed at seven o'clock.'

'It's all in the Gazette,' said George, 'See.'

'Excellent, thanks George. I also want to know exactly how the Lights get turned on – or off. Last night's power cut can't be a coincidence,' added Gracie. 'I'm sure that's part of Presto's plan.'

'We should go to the tram depot – that's where they build and store the illuminations,' said Violet. 'I know a couple of the fellas there from visiting with Pa. There's bound to be one who'll answer our questions.'

'Then I want to find out more about conjuring,' said Gracie. 'I think we should pay a visit to The Abracadabra.'

'There is one person we should speak to first,' said Phyllis. 'Audrey Mosson. We need to let her know that Presto's going to try and steal the tiara. I wouldn't like her to come to any harm.'

'You're right,' said Gracie. 'We need to find her, and quickly.'

'Well luckily the Gazette has also printed her itinerary,' said George. 'She's sightseeing with her pa all day.'

They peered at the article. Gracie grinned, 'Who fancies a trip to the Pleasure Beach this afternoon?'

'Me!' replied everyone.

'This is what we need to do,' said Gracie.

Chapter Thirteen

The Race To Find Audrey

It started to rain as the five of them walked towards the amusement park. Gracie didn't mind; the Pleasure Beach would be quieter if it was wet. She really hated crowds.

'I hope we can find Audrey,' said Gracie, as they walked through the white welcoming arch into a world of colour; whizzing, spinning, whirling machines of wonder everywhere she looked. Rollercoaster tracks criss-crossed over and under each other above her head, their wooden frames stretching to the cloudy sky in huge sweeping curves.

Gracie gazed up at *Noah's Ark*; the large boat rocking back and forth, lined with sculpted animals. 'We can always shelter in there if this rain carries on,' she joked.

'Oh no,' said Tom. 'I hate the ark.'

'I was only kidding,' said Gracie, distracted by a movement over by a stall where you could win teddy bears.

'Tom froze at the top of the staircase last time,' said Violet. 'I reckon he's afraid to step into the ark in case he falls off!'

'It's not that. I had to stop. My feet got soaked on those silly stepping stones. Ruined my best shoes.'

Gracie sensed movement again. She turned and saw someone moving closer. They were writing in a notebook and peering over the top of it, now and again. It was Miss Steele!

The others were still chatting.

'I like the ark,' said Violet. 'All those creepy dark corridors, and that part where the cow swishes her tail. Makes me jump out of my skin every time!'

'If you like frights, we should go on the *Ghost Train*,' said Phyllis. 'It's proper scary! There are all these faces looming out at you in the dark, and cobwebs dangling in your hair – and there's a giant spider!'

'Don't react,' said Gracie, 'but Miss Steele is over there – no, don't turn around George. She's writing in one of her notebooks again. I think she's spying on us.'

'Do you think she's working for the Prestons?' asked Violet.

'I don't know, but I don't want her following us. We can't have anyone knowing our plans. We need to shake her off!'

'Let's make a run for it,' whispered Tom.

'She might give chase,' said Phyllis.

'Not in those shoes, surely,' said Violet. 'Honestly, I don't know why women wear heels.'

'We need to split up,' said Gracie. 'When I say, we all scarper in opposite directions. Once you know you're not being tailed we'll meet up again.'

'But where?' said George. 'I don't know where all the rides are.'

'*The Grand National*,' said Tom.

'You can't miss it,' agreed Violet, subtly pointing with her thumb. 'It's that new rollercoaster other there with the big white column.'

'On the count of three – one, two, three!'

The children whizzed away. Gracie headed towards the *Big Dipper* and the boating lake. She ducked between stands selling ice cream and candy floss, her heart racing.

After a few minutes, sure she wasn't being followed, she made her way to *The Grand National.*

People were waiting in an orderly queue at the ride's station, but they seemed to be waiting on both sides of the platform. As Gracie got closer, she realized why. There were two tracks and two trains – although they didn't really look like trains. In fact, they looked more like sleds! The carriages were open fronted, with panels only along the sides.

She needed to blend in, in case Miss Steele was about.

She joined the back of the queue.

Around the railings were other people, who were enjoying just watching. Gracie scanned their faces, looking for her friends and George.

There was a tap on her shoulder. 'I think we lost her,' said Violet, grinning.

'Phew, we can carry on looking for Audrey, but we need to keep our eyes peeled for Miss Steele too.'

'Here's Tom,' Violet beckoned her brother over.

'And here comes George,' said Gracie, relieved. She waved him over. 'We're just waiting on Phyllis now.' The queue was moving forward.

'There she is!' said Tom. 'Look, she's in front of us!'

'Phyllis!' called Gracie.

The maid waved. 'Sorry, I thought Miss Steele had seen me. I had no choice but to merge into the queue.'

'We might as well get on too,' said Violet. 'We can't let poor Phyllis ride alone.'

'But I don't want to sit on a wet seat,' George complained. 'I'm not walking around with a soggy bottom, folk will think I've had an accident!'

'George!' wailed Gracie. 'You're obsessed. I swear, if you mention wee one more time!'

They shunted closer and closer to the pay booth. 'Look, the seats are dry any road,' said Tom, 'and it's stopped raining.'

They bought their tickets and stepped on to the platform.

'Over here, Phyllis,' called Gracie, beckoning her.

'Let's make this really fun and have a competition! Us girls will take the left side,' said Violet. 'You boys can take the right.'

George was flapping his arms at a seagull that had landed clumsily next to them. 'Hey, Gracie, it's the one you rescued! It must be following you. Hello, Gully!'

She couldn't believe it. It did seem to be the same seagull. 'It's probably a bit disorientated after being captured by Presto. Leave it be, George.'

'Look, here come our trains,' said Phyllis.

'It's the green one!' clapped George.

'I could have told you *that* three minutes ago,' said Violet. 'It's the way the ride works, see. If you start the ride on the right, you finish it on the left side. People are always trying to work out where the tracks swap over, but they don't. It's because it's a Möbious loop . . .'

'Nobody's interested, Vi. Folk just want to win the race!' said Tom, getting into the carriage.

'Well then, they need to work out which side is the heaviest,' added Violet, getting in. 'Which is why I've chosen the left side.'

Gracie sat down beside her, already feeling a bit nervous. Phyllis got into the carriage behind them.

The ride operator walked along the carriages. 'Stay seated at all times and hold on tight.' His eyes lingered on Gracie's arm, and she was glad when he didn't pass comment.

She held on to the metal bar in front. Suddenly, the klaxon sounded – and they were off!

The train rattled along the track as they pulled away from the station. The carriages rocked a little from side to side as they began to bend round to the left, and then the track rose steeply ahead of them.

The other train appeared to their right-hand side. Tom and George were in the carriage, level pegging with them. Violet and her brother held out their hands to touch each other as the chain lift pulled the twin carriages upwards. Everyone in the other carriages was doing the same.

'We're going to beat you!' George called out over the sound of the grinding mechanism, as their carriage pulled away.

'See you at the finish line, slow coach,' replied Gracie, laughing.

'Is it very fast?' asked Phyllis, leaning forward.

'Fifty miles per hour!' replied Violet. 'We're going to zoom past them any minute!'

They passed under an overhead sign reading: *THEY'RE OFF.*

Once they had reached the summit, the trains curved to the left and then suddenly fell away into a big scooping drop. Gracie screamed . . . down, down, down! Her hair whipped against her face and her cries became one with the other riders'.

The carriage rattled and vibrated furiously as it followed

the track's humps and twists. First, the train charged through *Becher's Brook*, then took a bend to the right. Gracie leaned into Violet for stability and gave a whoop as the carriage sped down again in undulating waves, reaching *Valentine's*. Gracie gritted her teeth as the track bent back on itself and continued up and down, feeling her stomach rise and fall with every drop. Then, the train reached *Canal Turn* and curved around again, beginning to catch up with the other train.

After another last couple of dips – the *Winning Post* came into view, straight ahead.

'Come on!' shouted Violet, as their carriage shot past her brother's.

They pulled first into the station. The girls had done it!

***

'That was amazing,' said Gracie, as they exited the station, 'but we're still no nearer to finding Audrey Mosson.'

'We could take a trip on the Pleasure Beach Express,' said Tom. 'The train goes around the whole amusement park.'

'Good idea,' said Phyllis, grinning. 'We might find the Railway Queen there too! Get it – *trains, Railway Queen*?'

'The Pleasure Beach Express's track is far too low – we wouldn't be able to see much at all,' said Violet, 'also it's a bit slow. No, what we need is height and speed – and I know just where to find it!' she added, eyes twinkling. 'To the planes!'

'Planes?' repeated Gracie, but her friend was already running.

'What is she on about?' she called as they all chased after her.

They skirted around the crowds, until they had reached a concrete building with the words: *Hiram Maxim's Flying Machines* on it.

Gracie looked high above her head. The ride was built on the flat roof of a large shop and consisted of a steel-lattice tower with ten metal boom arms outstretched: a plane at each end.

'They're supposed to be biplanes,' said Violet, leading them up the steps and on to the roof of the emporium. 'Except they only have an upper wing. Look – they have a pretend tiller at the back, but the propellers at the front actually spin!'

Tom rolled his eyes.

'Let's do girls versus boys again,' said George. 'There's not room in the plane for all five of us.'

They made their way to the front of the queue, where the ride operator who was dressed in a smart white jacket with red lapels and cuffs, would direct them to an empty plane.

It was their turn at last. Gracie stepped forward.

'Sorry miss, you can't go on,' he said, his eyes lingering on her left arm.

Gracie felt sick with embarrassment.

'It's the rules for this ride,' he added, staring at the floor now. 'You must be able to hold on with both hands, you see.'

'Oh, how ridiculous,' said Violet. 'Gracie can grip tightly enough with one hand.'

Gracie didn't want to argue. She could feel the rest of the queue looking at her. Some of the people were whispering.

'I'll wait for you downstairs,' she said.

'Are you sure?' asked Phyllis.

'If Gracie can't ride, none of us will,' said Tom.

'Thanks Tom, but it's important we find Audrey.' Plus they'd all paid for ride tickets and she could see that Violet was desperate to have a go in the planes. 'Any road, if you do see her, you can shout to me and I can get a head start.'

'You are clever,' said Phyllis.

Gracie blushed. 'See you in a bit.' She hurried downstairs, her face still feeling flushed. She found a bench to sit on and watched as her friends waited for their voyage to begin.

The pole in the centre of the tower began to rotate – and the planes began to slowly circle sixty feet above ground.

Gracie noticed other passengers were waving to family and friends below. *So much for having to hold on with both hands,* she thought.

The planes were picking up speed and they began to tilt to one side as they swung out further and further away from the platform. It seemed like they'd been going around for ages! The faster the planes circled, the harder it was to spot which plane George, Violet, Tom and Phyllis were in. Gracie just hoped they could spot Audrey from high up.

The sun cast shadows of the planes across the floor. She

watched them for a while, before deciding to walk around the base of the ride and past the shop. The planes were going too fast for her friends to wave to her now, and she doubted they could shout either.

'Out of the way, out of the way,' boomed a male voice ahead of her. Gracie wondered what all the fuss was about. She stepped out from under the canopy to see a man in a long black coat cutting through the crowds like he was Moses parting the Red Sea.

'It's her!' cried Gracie, as a photographer began to snap pictures of a young girl in a pale blue dress.

Chapter Fourteen

The Fun House

A udrey Mosson was heading towards a modern white building with the name *Fun House* spelled out on it on circular signs that swivelled from side to side.

The man in the coat sat on a bench nearby while Audrey Mosson went to the pay booth. It seemed she was going into the attraction alone.

This could be my chance to speak to the Railway Queen, thought Gracie. *Although, what if the Fun House is jam-packed? What if I panic?*

She couldn't risk losing Audrey Mosson, so she took a deep breath and sprinted towards the entrance. A strange laughter bellowed out. She turned to see a large glass case containing a mechanical man in a smart suit, rocking back and forth and laughing hysterically. *'Ha, ha, ha, ha, ha!'*

'Oh, shut up,' she whispered. She handed over her money at the pay booth and stepped inside.

The fun house was like a giant indoor obstacle course. Luckily, she couldn't see anyone in front of her. First, Gracie made her way along the corridor as quickly as she could to try and catch up with Audrey Mosson. A blast of air shot up from below, shocking her. She was glad she wasn't wearing a skirt.

Next, she had to weave around a double wall of barrels that threatened to topple over as she made her way through them.

'You can do this,' she told herself.

Whoosh! Another jet of air came blasting up from the next floor. It was like being under attack! Gracie hurried on, reaching out for the railing to keep her balance as she crossed over an inflated cushion. She struggled to keep upright as the floor squished and wobbled. Gracie giggled; it was like walking on a blancmange!

The next section of floor tilted like a seesaw, suddenly tipping her forwards, but the next section was even trickier. Gracie stepped on to two parallel planks; the left slid back as the right went forward, then in reverse. It was like being on skis! She raised her arms to keep her balance and continued onwards.

At last, Gracie reached the top of a multi-coloured staircase with deep steps.

She continued on to the right-hand side and clutched the

banister. The steps were snaking from side to side and bobbing up and down like ocean waves.

She trod carefully, each step falling away as Gracie stood on it, her stomach churning. She forced herself to go on – for Ma's sake.

The final steps were ordinary, but her legs were still trembling. She was very glad to reach the bottom of the staircase.

Her relief turned to dismay as she saw there were people at this lower level.

She was standing at the bottom of a massive slide with deep rises and falls, and surrounded by roundabouts. There were children everywhere!

Could one of them be the Railway Queen?

She paced the room, scanning for a pale blue dress, and then started to climb the stairs to the slide for a better look.

There! Audrey Mosson was spinning round and round in a roundabout.

'Miss Mosson!' she called out, but her voice was lost among the screams of pleasure from those using the play equipment.

Gracie turned around and pushed past those still trying to go up. She hurried after Audrey Mosson into a new part of the *Fun House*.

'Miss Mosson!' she called again. She was so close!

Gracie was suddenly twizzled the wrong way around and stepped on to a revolving circle hidden in the floor. 'Oh no!' she cried.

She stumbled off. A flash of pale blue! Audrey was getting out of the other side of a huge cylinder. Gracie would have to go through, but it wasn't going to be easy. It was like a spinning barrel on its side.

She put one foot in, and then the other. *It's not too bad*, she thought, but then took another step and lost her balance. 'Ahh!' she cried out, as she dropped to the floor with a smack.

Gracie glanced around to make sure no one was laughing at her.

She tried to get up again, but it was hopeless. She was sliding around, and she couldn't get enough of a push on her right hand.

Gracie attempted to control her breathing and rolled on to her front, so she could use her whole body to try and crawl to the edge of the cylinder, but the surface was too slippery, and she was getting tired. She closed her eyes for a moment to gather herself.

When she reopened them, she noticed that someone was standing at the entrance to the cylinder. They stretched out a hand.

It was Tom.

'We saw you run int' *Fun House*,' he explained, as Gracie clambered out and dusted herself down.

'I found Audrey Mosson – but now I've lost her again,' said Gracie, looking around at the roundabouts and spinning floors.

George, Violet and Phyllis had also caught up with her.

She felt better having them all at her side.

'We should split up, so we can find her,' began Gracie.

She noticed that George was bouncing up and down and pointing over her shoulder. 'Look!' he cried.

Gracie span around to see the Railway Queen sliding down the huge slide in the middle of the *Fun House*.

'Woohoo!' shouted Audrey Mosson, as she zoomed to the bottom.

'Quick!' cried Gracie, running across the room, the others at her heel.

The Railway Queen was sitting at the bottom, giggling.

'Excuse me, Miss Mosson,' said Gracie, trying to think of the right words, while all around her was screams and laughter.

Audrey looked up. 'Have you been on this slide? It's spectacular! Although it does burn your bum a bit!'

'She said bum,' whispered George in awe.

'Shh, George,' said Gracie, 'Miss Mosson, my name is Gracie Fairshaw and these are my friends. This is Violet, Tom and Phyllis.'

'Please, call me Audrey,' she held out her hand, and they all shook it in turn. 'Must be much more fun being at the fair with your pals. Daddy doesn't like going on rides, so I've had to pick things I can do on my own. I really wanted to go on *The Reel*, but it's best to be part of a group. I don't suppose you would go on it with me?'

Gracie smiled and looked to the others.

'Of course,' they said as one.

'Splendid,' replied Audrey, clapping her hands. 'I always say that Blackpool is the friendliest town.'

They made their way out of the *Fun House* and walked across to *The Reel*. Gracie looked up at the ride, which was designed to look like the side of a mountain with a track that zig-zagged from the summit.

'This will have to be my last ride,' said Audrey. 'I've been invited to switch on the Illuminations later.'

'Actually, that's why we wanted to speak to you,' said Gracie, 'but we'll explain more when we're on *The Reel*.'

There was no queue, so they were able to get straight into one of the big, round carriages.

Everyone piled in, boys first, then the girls. There was just room for them all. The ride operator in his smart white jacket started to push the great carriage up the track.

'Be careful,' said the man. 'Hold on tight.'

Gracie and the others lay an arm around the back of the carriage and gripped the safety rail. She kept her left arm tucked close to her body and squished up next to Violet, hoping the operator wouldn't notice.

'Sometimes I think it would be easier to put my arm in a sling,' Gracie whispered to her friend. 'People have sympathy for you if you break your arm, but they can treat you very strangely if you happen to have been born with half of one.

'Do people stare a lot?' asked Audrey, as a second operator helped push the carriage to the base of the hill lift.

Gracie nodded. 'I'm not sure which is worse, the ones who make nasty comments and jokes, or the ones who fuss over me as though I'm a baby. They can't see that I'm just the same as them. I don't want pity or special consideration. I'm just a girl the same as you, or Phyllis or Violet, but some folk can't see that.'

Audrey nodded.

The chain underneath the track began to pull them up the hill.

'Friendship is very important isn't it, Audrey?' commented Violet. 'Friends help each other, you understand that.'

'Oh yes,' said Audrey.

'That's why we have agreed to help Gracie,' said Tom. 'You see, she's uncovered a plot to spoil the Switch-On tonight.'

'*No,*' gasped Audrey, as the carriage neared the summit.

'Yes, there is supposed to be a performance by Hey Presto! just before you press the button to turn the Lights on,' said Tom.

'He's kidnapped our ma,' said George, 'so he can force her to assist him.'

'He's a conman conjurer and he's really planning to turn *out* the lights,' said Gracie.

The carriage began to tip on to the downward track 'Oh,

how absolutely aaawwfffuulll!' yelled Audrey as *The Reel* began to plummet.

Everyone screamed as the round carriage hurtled along, flying from side to side and spinning after every bend, making Gracie feel a bit sick.

It was hard to keep up any conversation, but Gracie did her best. 'We're glad you think so, because we need your help,' she continued, her jaw rattling.

The Reel was beginning to slow as it reached the bottom and was now doing its final swirls. 'We'll put Phyllis in your place, so we can catch Presto red-handed as he tries to steal your tiara.'

'Why would Presto want my tiara?' asked Audrey, as the ride came to a final stop.

Gracie was confused. 'Because it's worth a fortune.'

Audrey burst out laughing. 'My tiara?'

'Yes, your diamond tiara,' repeated Gracie.

Audrey was staring at her like she was mad.

'*Diamond*?' She laughed again.

Gracie scowled. 'What's so funny?'

'Oh dear,' said Audrey, chewing her lip. 'My tiara's not real.'

Chapter Fifteen
The Tiara Trap

The gang all climbed out of the carriage. Tears began to well in Gracie's eyes, and there was nothing she could do to stop them.

'I'm so sorry,' said Audrey softly, passing over a handkerchief. 'My tiara is only costume jewellery – a bit of shiny metal with pieces of cut glass glued on.'

George wrapped an arm around his sister. 'We should have known they wouldn't put diamonds on top of a fifteen-year-old Miss Blackpool.'

'She's the Railway Queen, not Miss Blackpool,' said Gracie between sobs.

'I would still like to help you,' said Audrey. 'Presto doesn't know my tiara is fake, does he?'

'That's true,' said Gracie. 'I mean, it fooled us.'

'We could ask the League of the Shining Star to be on red alert,' said Tom, opening his satchel and taking out a pen and paper. 'We just need to replace Auntie Astra's letter with one of our own.'

'We've only a couple of hours until the Gazette's deadline,' said Violet. 'Write this down.'

Dear League of the Shining Star,

Many of you will be at tonight's Switch-On when Audrey Mosson, the Railway Queen, will light up the Illuminations for another season.

As members of the League of the Shining Star, you have vowed to be kind and decent, fair and honest. We make our sign to remember our pledge. Our sign is a symbol to come together and fight evil.

Tonight, the League must shine as bright at Blackpool.

Love, Auntie Astra

'I can drop the letter off for you,' said Audrey. 'Then we should meet up at the Town Hall. If you can come over for four o'clock, you'll be able to watch the run-through. We have to have a practice so it all goes smoothly. I'm ever so nervous. Even more so now I know about Presto's plan.'

'Don't worry, we'll be there,' said Gracie. 'With any luck, Presto will want to practice his part in the ceremony an' all.'

***

Phyllis opened The Majestic's front door. Gracie, George, Tom and Violet trooped in behind her.

'I've got to get on in the kitchen,' said Phyllis, 'I'm making a few sandwiches for lunch and I've got a hotpot to cook. We'll have it after the Switch-On. There's not many guests left now, so it should do us all.' She headed to the Fairshaw's private quarters.

Gracie and the others went into the parlour. Miss Steele had her notebook out, while the Hill sisters were playing a game of draughts.

'Oh look, it's Gully!' said George, wandering over to the front window. 'He's followed us.'

'Who's Gully?' asked Tom.

'Gracie's pet seagull,'

'Don't be ridiculous, George. That seagull is not my pet.'

'Gully thinks he is,' George replied, 'see.'

Gracie span around. He wasn't kidding. The bird was staring in through the window. 'It's just looking for food.'

'It's looking for you,' said George, crossly. 'You might as well accept it.'

Gracie drew the curtains. 'There, it will go now.'

George snuck over and peered through a slight gap in them. 'Gully's still waiting for you.'

Violet and Tom laughed.

'It's probably roosting,' replied Gracie. 'Now, come away from there!'

George sighed and did as he was told. He picked up a pack of cards, shuffled the deck and shared them out. 'We're playing pontoon,' he said.

Gracie couldn't help overhearing the sisters' conversation as they sat down to play.

'They reckon 70,000 people are coming in on the trains for the Switch-On,' said Edna to Elspeth. 'The trams will be heaving.'

70,000! Gracie gave an involuntary shudder at the thought of all those people gathered in one spot.

'I've ordered a taxi to take me into town later. You're welcome to share it with me, ladies,' said Miss Steele.

'That's very kind of you dear, thank you,' said Elspeth.

'Very kind,' added Edna.

'I suppose you'll be leaving this weekend too,' said Elspeth.

'Indeed. I must head back to London and write up my report. It's been fascinating watching the Milltowners in Blackpool.'

'Are . . . are you a spy?' asked Gracie.

'Ha! That day may come,' replied Miss Steele. 'I am a mass observer, part of a special department that has been drafted to study the lives of ordinary people; the working class. I have to record everything, conversations, activity, relationships . . .'

'So, your notebook – you use it to record everyone's movements?' asked Gracie. That was why she had been watching people at the Pleasure Beach and in The Majestic!

'That's right,' replied Miss Steele. 'See, here I write down the name of the guest I am observing, and then here I record the time, what they are doing and anything they say.'

'Dinner is ready,' said Phyllis, appearing at the parlour door.

Gracie and the guests stood and made their way to the dining room. Miss Steele's notebooks would make excellent evidence.

The maid had piled the sideboard up with sandwiches, quartered pork pies and cold boiled eggs.

Gracie made George and her friends wait while the guests plated up. Once they had finished, she picked up a plate and moved it nearer to the food choices, adding a boiled egg, a piece of pie and a handful of plain crisps to her plate. She carried it to a table away from the remaining guests.

George was trying to build a mountain of buffet on his own plate. He had made a tower of ham sandwiches and was trying to balance a whole pie on top.

Gracie settled herself, then picked up her piece of pie and bit into the crisp, buttery pastry. The meat had a thin layer of gelatine on top. It was perfection.

Phyllis came out of the back kitchen, carrying a bowl of trifle.

'Ooh, lovely,' said the Hill sisters. 'What a treat.'

George quickly created a mountain of crusts on his plate and greedily eyed up the trifle.

The Hill sisters were already making short work of the jelly and cream dessert.

'I hope we don't get indigestion!' said Edna, licking her spoon.

Gracie grinned. In a short time, she'd grown fond of the old ladies. It was funny to think she'd been worried about sharing her new home with strangers, but she could see that it could be fun having lots of different types of people staying over. Even in the despair of Ma's absence, she could see the good in folk. She was sorry that Edna had lost her necklace and wished there was a way to get it back, but Mrs Preston and the pendant were probably miles away by now.

'We'll do the dishes,' said Gracie, 'you've done enough for us, Phyllis. Get yourself some dinner.'

The maid blew air into her fringe, 'I could do with a break. I'm going to sit in the parlour for a bit.'

Gracie and George had the task of washing and Tom and Violet had drying. Sometimes George scrubbed while Gracie held the crockery – and sometimes they did the opposite. There was a familiarity to the routine that was comforting, but it was fun to have Tom and Violet alongside, flicking each other with their tea towels and scooping bubbles on to each other's head.

Once they had finished, Violet checked her watch. 'Right, let's go to the tram depot first,' she said, 'we can ask the men there if they've heard of The Abracadabra. The drivers know Blackpool like the back of their hand.'

Chapter Sixteen

Secrets

Once the clean dishes were put away, the gang grabbed their coats. Gracie picked up her shoulder bag, while George suddenly disappeared into the kitchen.

He came back with a large chunk of cheese and a thick slice of bread. He pushed them into his pocket.

On the way out, they popped their heads around the parlour door to tell Phyllis they'd be back around 5 p.m. to help with tea. Then they headed out and along Osborne Road to catch a tram.

This time, they got off at Rigby Road and waited for a stream of cars to pass so they could cross over the promenade.

They followed the curving tram lines to the tram depot. The yard was surrounded by tall fencing, but Violet knew the way in.

Gracie stepped across a pool of oil and followed her friend towards a row of brick hangars with painted green woodwork.

'Over there are the workshops for repairing motors, bodywork and for fitting out the trams,' said Violet. 'Isn't it brilliant!'

'I'll take George to see the trams while you go with Gracie to the Illuminations workshop,' said Tom. 'We'll ask the drivers if they've heard of The Abracadabra.'

Gracie and Violet headed to an old wooden aircraft hangar with the words 'Carnival Shop' painted on it.

Gracie scrunched up her nose in confusion, but when they entered the hangar, she saw large sections of Illuminations tableau secured to trellis fencing, boxes of bulbs and tins of paint.

A man in a paint-splattered overcoat hollered as they entered. 'Woah!' he called, running across to stop them. 'Oh, it's only you, Miss Emberton. Is your father with you?'

Violet grinned. 'Hi Bill. No, don't panic – everything's fine with the Switch-On. Actually, he wanted me out of his hair for a few hours, so I thought I'd show my friend around the depot, if I'm allowed? Gracie is new to Blackpool and she's completely fascinated by the Illuminations.'

'I can see why she's your friend,' said Bill, grinning, as he pulled his glasses down from his forehead on to his nose. His eye line settled for a moment on Gracie's arm. 'I could give you both a short tour if you like, it'll be safer that way. We've got animated tableaux coming in for emergency repairs, there's a storm forecast and I'm worried one or two of them won't stand a battering.'

The air smelled of fresh paint and wood shavings. Gracie admired some large wooden fairies. She noticed holes had been drilled into the wood, and a couple of men were now fastening lights into them.

'Let's start in my office,' said Bill.

The walls were covered in blueprints and beautiful neon-pastel designs on black paper. Gracie studied a series of sketches that depicted a dapper gentleman and a terrier dog.

'They're my ideas for next year's season,' said Bill, dragging out a chair. 'It'll be all change in 1936. Rumour is we'll be splitting from the tram department and moving into the yard by the old stables! The good news is, they reckon we will have a core staff of twelve working exclusively on the Lights. Still, that's the way with Blackpool – our motto is *progress*, after all!'

He rummaged in his desk drawer. 'Ah, here's a special Gazette souvenir all about this year's Lights.' He flicked through the pages. 'There are some early photographs here you'll find interesting.

'The Illuminations began in 1879, of course there were only eight arc electric lights then, but this was when streets were lit by gas. Thousands came to see them from across the country! So, when the first royal visit to Blackpool was planned in 1912, the town decided to light up Princess Parade with 10,000 bulbs.

After the war, it was decided the lights would be brought back. You can keep that brochure if you like.'

'Thank you,' said Gracie.

'Right, let's go into the workshop.' Bill pointed to a string of lights stretching across the ceiling as they made their way around the hangar. 'We call this *Festoon* – it is used to illuminate buildings, columns and arches.'

'It's very pretty,' said Gracie.

'We still use a lot of it, but now we have the animated tableaux,' Bill pointed to the larger panels with the cut outs. 'We fix lamps – that's the proper word for them, not bulbs – into the holes; sometimes we paint them to make them coloured, and then we fit them with electrical contacts. Here, let me show you.'

He led Gracie and Violet across to a large cylinder. 'This is a mechanical light sequencer. There's a motor to drive a gearbox. The cylinder is mounted with copper strips, each with a corresponding brass finger.'

'Ah, I get it,' said Violet. 'As the cylinder rotates, it makes or breaks the connection –causing the lamp to turn on and off.'

'Exactly, we can lengthen the copper strips to adjust the timings. With our new fairy-tale displays, it gives the effect of the picture moving. For example, the mouse running up *Hickory Dickory Clock.*'

'What about the Switch-On?' asked Gracie. 'When the button is pressed, does that send an electric current to all the lamps?'

'Ha! Wouldn't that be something! No, we've not reached that level of technology yet. The Switch-On column is linked to the lights on the Town Hall only. When they illuminate, engineers will each turn on their section.'

'So, if the contact failed, the lights would go out in Talbot Square?' asked Violet.

'That's right in theory, Miss Emberton,' replied Bill, 'but the engineers check every lamp and every connection to ensure that doesn't happen.'

Gracie noticed Tom and George at the entrance to the depot. 'Well, thank you for the tour, it's been fascinating.'

'Really useful,' said Violet, checking her watch, 'but we'd better be going now. Tom and I have to meet Pa for the run-through.'

***

'Did you find out where The Abracadabra is?' asked Gracie, as they re-joined the boys.

'Most of the drivers hadn't heard of it,' replied Tom, 'luckily, we found one whose son is interested in conjuring. He said it's a magic shop just off Corporation Street.'

***

It only took about twenty minutes to reach the town centre. They soon spotted a large board with an 'A' and a picture of a magic wand on it at the entrance to a slim alleyway.

The Abracadabra was a tall, narrow building with drawn-down black blinds. The door bore no number, but the top of each window was a stained-glass image of a magic wand sparking coloured flames.

Gracie found the doorbell and pressed it. A musical melody rang out.

A boy of about sixteen, wearing an orange turban opened the door. 'Welcome to The Abracadabra,' he said. 'My name is Deepu. How can I be of assistance today?'

They followed him along a long corridor that was decorated with colourful illustrated posters of conjurers.

He turned into the room on the right and made his way behind a long glass counter. It was filled with small props. There was an assortment of playing cards, steel rings, paper flowers, coins and coloured spheres.

'Are you looking for anything in particular?' asked Deepu. 'We have three floors of illusions and magic props – everything from rope to rabbits.'

'We want information,' said George.

'We have a good number of books for sale . . .' said Deepu, indicating several shelves behind him, filled with leather-bound books.

'We want to learn the art of conjuring,' said Gracie. 'The principles of some basic tricks.'

'Ha!' said Deepu. 'Even basic tricks take hours and hours of practice.' He tapped the side of his nose. 'Are you asking me to break the Conjurer's Code? To share the secrets of my profession with strangers?'

'Yes,' said Violet. She held her hand aloft and clenched and unclenched her fist.

Deepu grinned and returned the gesture. 'Why didn't you say you were in the League? What do you need to know?'

'If you wanted to make summat disappear – how would you do it?' asked Gracie.

'Well, there are different categories of illusion,' Deepu explained. 'There's Transformation – making something change into a different object. Transportation – when you make something move to a different place, such as a coin or the conjurer's assistant. Production – making something from nothing, like when a dove or a playing card appears out of thin air.

'Then there's Levitation – that's defying gravity. Solid-through-solid – steel rings are a good example, or a man walking into a mirror.

'Prediction – that's mind reading. Restoration – cutting or smashing an object that becomes whole again, such as sawing a woman in half . . . and finally, Vanish – that's the technique for making something or someone disappear.'

Deepu put his hands into the counter and pulled out three cups and a ball. 'Of course, the more complex tricks use a number of the methods. Now watch . . .'

He performed at speed. The ball appeared on top of a cup

before he seemingly pushed it through the lid – and when he lifted the cup, the ball was already underneath. Then Deepu made the ball move from cup to cup, where it became two balls, and then three, before they all disappeared.

'Now, check your bag,' said Deepu, grinning at Gracie.

Gracie opened her bag. All three balls were inside!

Gracie clapped her hand against her arm and the others joined in. She passed the balls to Deepu.

'One illusion can use a combination of vanishes, production, solid-through-solid, teleportation and transformation,' he explained.

'I thought that was all just sleight-of-hand,' said Tom.

'*Just?*' said Deepu. 'The art of legerdemain requires great dexterity, psychology, timing, misdirection and skilled choreography.'

'So, all those skills would be required for a vanish too?' asked Gracie.

'Of course,' Deepu replied, 'but the key ingredient to a successful vanish is preparation. The conjurer will have carefully planned their position on stage, along with the audience's view. He may have also commissioned a special piece of equipment; a chair with a seat that drops the lady through a trap door, for example.

'Other vanishes depend on mirrors. The conjurer opens a cabinet and his assistant climbs inside. Once the doors are closed, the assistant unhooks two secret hinged mirrors that are camouflaged to look like the cabinet interior. She hides at the back of the cabinet and brings the two mirrors together to form a triangle. When the cabinet is opened, the audience believes the assistant has vanished – thanks to mathematics and reflection.'

Gracie rubbed her chin, 'Because people can't really disappear.'

'Exactly,' replied Deepu. 'They can only be hidden.'

Chapter Seventeen

The Switch

They decided to show their thanks to Deepu by buying something each. George selected a box with a finger in it, Violet picked a rubber pencil and tucked it behind her ear, and Tom opted for a silk handkerchief – though Gracie suspected it was only for his pocket.

'Will you be at the Switch-On tonight?' asked Gracie, while paying for a pack of cards for herself.

'Oh yes, didn't you see the message on Auntie Astra's page? All the League has been told to go!'

They exited the shop and walked north towards the Town Hall. The streets were already getting busier. Gracie hooked her arm through Violet's.

They could hear car horns beeping on the promenade as they neared Talbot Square.

'It's this new one-way system for the Illuminations,' said Violet. 'It's supposed to keep the traffic flowing, but it must be causing terrible confusion.'

Tom clapped his hands to his eyes. 'No one cares!'

The Town Hall, with its pink brick and stone bay windows, was on the corner.

They made their way past and crossed over, so they were facing the front entrance.

A purpose-built platform had been constructed in front of it. A line of ordinary looking men were sitting on a row of chairs at the back. *They must be stand-ins for the councillors and other invited guests*, Gracie thought.

Mr Emberton was standing at the microphone. 'I have been looking forward, as Mayor and Chairman of the Electricity Committee, to switching on the Illuminations et cetera, et cetera.' He nodded, apparently satisfied with the sound.

'When does Presto appear?' asked George.

'We'll have to wait and see,' said Gracie.

Mr Emberton nodded to the side of the stage. Audrey Mosson stepped up to the platform.

'Stop, stop!' Mr Emberton pointed at a thick electric lead that was trailing across the floor. 'Find me an engineer!' he snapped, his words echoing out across the square.

A man in dungarees appeared from the side of the platform. He dropped a holdall bag on to the ground, then went over to inspect the lead.

Violet was watching his every move. Gracie was sure that it would be her friend called upon to fix things, one day.

There was a sudden movement out of the corner of Gracie's eye. They weren't the only ones watching the engineer.

'He's here,' said Gracie. Fortunately, Presto was so focused on the activity in front of the Town Hall that he hadn't cast a glance in their direction.

Mr Emberton was discussing something with Presto, but the conjurer now seemed more interested in the road. He kept glancing at the entrance to Market Street, which ran up the other side of the Town Hall.

Gracie leaned to see what the distraction was.

A van was turning the corner and then parking up. She could just make out some of the lettering on its side. *Tower Removals*. Presto's conjuring equipment was being delivered.

'George, lend me your pen knife,' she said.

Her brother hesitated, then pulled it out of his pocket. 'What are you going to do with it?' he asked, his eyes wide.

'I'm going to break into Presto's van.'

'You're going to need better tools,' said Violet. 'Leave it to me . . .' She tucked her auburn plaits inside her woolly hat, then, head down, she walked towards the platform.

'Tom, keep an eye on George. I'm going to rescue Ma.'

'We'll come with you . . .' said Tom.

'No, I need you to keep an eye on Presto,' replied Gracie, 'In case he returns to his van before I'm done.'

'Be careful,' said Tom.

'I will be.' But Gracie's heart was racing as she strolled away from the Town Hall. At a safe distance, she crossed over and doubled back to Market Street. She went to the front of the van. The removals men were sitting inside.

Gracie put her hand in her pocket and took out some money.

The driver wound the window down. 'What do you want, love?'

'Mr Dixon said he's going to be a while, so you should go and get a cuppa. He said you should leave the keys in the ignition for him.'

'I told you they'd be hours setting up,' said the mate. 'Come on, you can have a cup of tea, I want something stronger.'

They got out of the van and headed down Market Street.

Gracie waited until they were out of sight, then opened the door and took the keys.

She hurried to the back of the van and undid the shutter lock. Gracie pushed the handle upwards and the shutter flew up.

'Ma? Are you in here?' she called. There was a little step for getting into the back of the van. Gracie clambered on to it, almost losing her balance.

The van was filled with illusions and animals as before. The doves cooed and the rabbit pawed at its cage.

'For my next trick,' trilled Sunny the budgie.

The conjurer's cabinet was at the back. It had been turned to face the wall and a chain was bound around it – a large padlock holding it in place.

She remembered Deepu's words. *People can't vanish.* She didn't know how Presto had concealed Ma up to now, but she was certain she was inside the cabinet this time. She didn't care if the trick had been done by Production or Transportation; the only thing that mattered was helping Ma escape.

'I'm here, Ma!' called Gracie. 'I'll get you out.'

Gracie thought she could hear a muffled voice and the sound of someone kicking a foot against wood. 'Mmm, mmm!' Ma was definitely in the cabinet!

'I've got it,' called a voice behind her.

Gracie turned. Violet heaved a large engineer's bag into the van and climbed in after it. 'I didn't know what we'd need, so I brought the lot.'

Gracie helped Violet drag the bag nearer to the cabinet. The girls opened it up and peered inside.

Violet pulled out a pair of bolt cutters. 'Let's not mess about trying to open the padlock.'

Gracie held the chain steady. The metal felt cold against her skin. 'Not long now, Ma.'

There was another kick against the wood. Violet squeezed hard with the bolt cutters, groaning with the effort.

'Please, Violet, keep trying,' begged Gracie.

Violet squeezed again. This time the cutters chopped through the link. The chain clattered to the floor.

'We need to turn it round,' said Gracie, 'to get to the doors.'

'No, look,' said Violet. 'See the way it's been decorated to look like two vertical pieces of wood put together with a metal strip between? I think this cabinet has a false back, that way an assistant can slip in or out of it – so they can vanish. I'll find a torch.'

Gracie stared at the wood. Was Violet right? She felt along the edges, discovering a discreet set of hinges. 'Ma, can you step to the left? Bang once for yes, twice for no.'

BANG! . . . and then a shuffling sound.

Gracie pushed hard against the cabinet, and the right side opened inwards as a door.

Violet shone a torch into the cabinet.

The light fell across Ma's face. Her mouth was gagged and her hands were bound together.

Gracie pulled out George's penknife and leaned in, so she could cut away at the rope.

She sawed back and forth, her wrist aching with the effort. Eventually the threads started to give, and Ma forced her hands apart, breaking the ties.

Gracie pulled the gag from her mouth. It was her handkerchief. She unfurled it – the letters A.F. taunted her. Presto must have found it and then used it in this horrific way.

Ma took deep gasps of air. 'Gracie, oh my clever girl. How did you ever find me?' she asked, with tears in her eyes.

'Careful,' said Gracie stepping back, as she guided her out of the cabinet.

'What time is it?' asked Ma. 'Where are we? Is it the Switch-On yet?'

'We're right next to the Town Hall,' explained Gracie. 'Don't worry, Presto will be a while yet. They were having some technical difficulties, and he's got to rehearse his part.'

'Sit here, Mrs Fairshaw,' said Violet, pointing to a large suitcase. 'I'll go and get some water.'

'My legs are like jelly,' said Ma, slumping on to the suitcase.

'You've been missing a day and a half,' Gracie tried to speak between loud sobs, as she sat next to her.

'Hey, I'm safe now, don't cry.' Ma took her hand.

'I couldn't find you,' wept Gracie. 'I kept looking, but you'd vanished. What happened Ma?'

'You remember I'd forgotten my glasses? Well, I was coming back down the corridor from our room with them,' explained Ma, 'when I heard someone being sick in the communal toilet. I knocked quietly and asked if they needed a doctor. Mrs Dixon moaned and told me to leave her alone, but I was worried about her, so I went over to their room and knocked on the door.'

'Mr Dixon's door – only he's not Mr Dixon, he's Peter

Preston.' Gracie stared at the ground. 'Is it true you were Presto's assistant, Ma?'

Ma nodded sadly. 'It was only for a short time. You see, I was your age when I met him,' she ran her fingers over the suitcase handle. 'We were both staying at The Majestic and I was flattered when he asked me to be his assistant, but I never agreed to trick people. I never stole from anybody. That's why we fell out, because I refused to help him con people.'

'So that's why he kidnapped you, because you threatened to reveal that he's a conman conjurer?' Gracie let out her breath. A mixture of relief and guilt swelled her chest. How could she have doubted her Ma? She wrapped her arm around her shoulder and squeezed.

'When Peter answered the door, it was like he'd been expecting me. "You've come," he said. "I knew you would."

'I told him his wife was ill, and that he should go to her, but he was just staring at me.' Ma blushed. 'He said I hadn't changed at all. "How funny that we were both drawn back to The Majestic after all these years."

'He didn't mention our big argument and my leaving him. I thought, well, we're both grown-ups now – people change. I asked him into our private quarters so I could find an address for a doctor, but once we were inside, he started talking about the old days and what a great partnership we'd been. How he was going to be doing a special appearance at the Switch-On, but he was worried that it was going to be a disaster. "My wife's a drunk," he said, "but it doesn't matter now you're here. I always knew you'd come back."

'I told him he was wrong. That I was a mother and a landlady now. That I would never be his assistant again. Peter was furious. There was a struggle . . .' said Ma. 'He was so much stronger than me. He clasped something over my mouth.'

'Your hanky,' said Gracie, clutching it tightly in her hand.

'Perhaps. Then Peter forced me out to his room, then through into the next one and shoved me into the wardrobe.'

'He still thinks he can force you to be his assistant?' said Gracie. 'That's why he's kidnapped you? Why he's brought you here?'

Ma nodded. 'Peter wants to turn back time, but I've told him even a conjurer can't do that.'

'We've got to get out of here,' said Gracie, pushing herself up. She held her hand out to Ma.

'I just need a minute,' said Ma, resting against the back of the van. 'I need to catch my breath.'

Mr Emberton's voice echoed out across the square, Gracie turned her head. 'Ladies and gentlemen, boys and girls, please welcome – Hey Presto! . . .'

Gracie cried out. Presto was not stepping on to the stage, he was running towards the van!

'Go, Gracie,' urged Ma. 'You can still raise the alarm.'

'Not without you . . .' Presto was getting nearer.

'I'm too tired – please, Gracie. Go.' She shunted her.

Gracie shook her head. 'I won't leave you, Ma.'

'You don't give up, do you?' sneered Presto, gasping for breath as he reached the van. He looked at Gracie, Ma and the cabinet. 'You have made the vanished lady reappear. Congratulations, conjuring talent must run in the family.'

'You don't know anything about me or my ma,' spat Gracie.

'Don't I?' Presto grinned, as he climbed inside. 'I know how important family is to both of you.' He crouched down in front of Gracie and Ma. 'How you would do anything for each other, or George.'

'George?' cried Ma.

'Don't worry,' scoffed Gracie. 'George is safe. My friend Tom is looking after him.'

'Are you sure about that?' said Presto, raising an eyebrow.

'He's trying to trick us, Ma.'

'I can't take that chance, Gracie.' She stared into Presto's eyes. 'What do you want?'

'You already know. I want an assistant to help me at the Switch-On.'

Ma took a deep breath. 'I'll do it, for the sake of my children.' She tried to get up.

'That's very kind of you, but you can hardly stand. No, I have a better idea,' said Presto. 'I want Gracie to be my assistant.'

Chapter Eighteen
Countdown

'Gracie can't be your assistant, Peter.' She doesn't know how any of your illusions are done. She doesn't know how to palm an object, or how to slip something into place, or how to manipulate her body so it can squeeze into confined spaces. You have to let me do it,' insisted Ma.

'No! You might try to sabotage my act or call out for help,' said Presto, 'but if I have Gracie *and* George under my control, then I know you will do whatever I say – and that starts with you staying in the van.'

Presto lifted the lid on a bright red trunk. He pulled out a short, gold-coloured dress with sequins and fringing all over it. He threw it at Gracie. 'You'll need shoes too.' He rummaged inside another box and pulled out a pair of silver heels. 'They've got straps, so it doesn't matter if they're too big.

Gracie scowled. 'What trick do you want me to help with? Pocketing an old lady's necklace or sleight of hand so you can steal a hard-working man's watch?'

'They were minor contributions to my living expenses,' said Presto. 'Now, Annie, don't worry, I promise to let you out again after the show, and then you can go back to your boring little life as a mother and a landlady.'

He pushed Gracie towards the back of the van and made her climb down, before doing the same and pulling down the shutter behind them.

Presto gripped Gracie's arm and bustled her towards the side entrance to the Town Hall.

I've got to go along with this until I can find a way out, she thought. *Violet will be back soon, she'll find Ma and raise the alarm that Presto has taken me.*

***

Gracie looked out of a Town Hall window on to Talbot Square below. She knew now that Violet hadn't gone back to the van or she would have been rescued. Something had gone wrong.

Her head was swimming with Presto's instructions. He had gone over his Switch-On performance with her again and again.

It's only one trick, she thought, *but if I get it wrong!* Gracie felt her stomach churn.

A huge crowd had already gathered in front of the platform, stretching as far as North Pier and up Talbot Street. She was dreading standing in front of all those people.

Her costume felt too clingy, and she felt chilled to the core despite the room's heating.

There was a knock on the door, and Presto entered. He had changed into his tuxedo and freshly slicked back his hair.

'I don't know why I didn't kidnap you in the first place. A one-armed assistant! The audience will be fascinated by you, Gracie. They won't be able to take their eyes off you! All the time they're staring at you, they won't be looking at me.

'Shall we go down?' he asked, as though she had a choice.

Gracie didn't reply. She followed him along the corridor, the sound of the crowd getting louder. She crossed the landing, before descending the grand wooden staircase past a large stained-glass window.

She ran her hand down the balustrade in order to steady herself, as they approached the foyer. Gracie glanced at the heraldic beasts and the statue of Queen Victoria and tried to feel braver.

Presto's instructions repeated in her mind as they made their way out of the Town Hall to the ceremony platform.

There was a large basket in the centre of the stage. Gracie swallowed hard. Her palm was sweaty, she wiped it against her costume, leaving a damp patch.

Gracie looked up at images of cherubs and strange dolphin-like creatures carved into the Town Hall's walls. Over the door were two carved figures, the one on the right holding the scales of justice – but there would be no justice brought against Presto.

She looked along the line of important-looking men, councillors and other officials seated at the back of the stage. Violet and Tom were sitting with their father. From the look on their faces, Mr Emberton was clearly telling them off. He must have spotted them during rehearsal, that must be why no one had come to her rescue.

There was no sign of George. Presto must have snatched him!

Even if Tom and Violet confided their plan to trap Preston to their pa, likely as not, he would dismiss their story, just like the constable had. Adults always believed grown-ups over children. If he did listen, he was still unlikely to do anything in the moments before the Switch-On. By the time he acted, Presto would be long gone.

The conjurer walked to the centre of the stage. 'I have travelled the globe looking for an illusion suitable for such a prestigious event as the Switch-On of the Blackpool Illuminations. I was taught how to levitate by a Cambodian princess, I learned how to read minds from a wise man in China and I was shown how to make a donkey disappear by a magician in Scarborough!'

The crowd laughed.

'They are child's play compared to what you will see tonight. The Sword of India.'

The crowd applauded.

169

Presto tilted the wicker basket and lifted the lid so the audience could see it was empty.

Gracie walked to the centre of the stage. Her eyes were blurred with silent tears. She had to trust that he would not hurt her, not in front of all these people.

She could hear the whispering as she reached the basket. She tried to shut out the sound as she stepped into it, the wicker material scratchy against her skin.

Presto produced a large silk sheet from up his sleeve and wafted it over her head, concealing her entirely from view. This was her cue to get into position. Gracie snaked down into the basket.

Quickly, she manoeuvred on to her side and coiled herself up tight. Her position had to be precise; Presto had made her practice again and again, getting more frustrated as time ticked on.

Gracie looked up at the lowering lid as it blocked out the fading sunlight.

Presto would be showing the swords to the crowd. She stiffened her body and waited for the first blade to pierce through the wicker near her head.

Her stomach churned as she heard it slice through the basket. Gracie gave a loud groan for effect.

The crowd gasped.

Gracie slowly fed the blunted blade in front of her body and out through the other side.

170

A second blade poked into the wicker by her feet, again she gave a groan, as she eased it safely across the inside of the basket and out of the other side.

The third and final blade penetrated the top of the lid. Gracie sucked in her stomach and guided the sword down.

The crowd burst into applause.

Presto was pulling the blades out again. Gracie kept perfectly still, knowing this part of the act was just as risky.

At last all three swords were removed, the lid was lifted and the silk sheet wafted overhead. Gracie twisted herself into a position so she could writhe up out of the basket to be revealed unharmed.

She blinked hard as she came back into the light. The material fell to the ground and she gave a bow.

Presto took her hand and she stepped out to enthusiastic clapping and cheering.

Gracie gave another bow, and then retreated to the side of the platform with the conjurer. Presto's next instructions filled her mind. 'The Railway Queen makes her speech. There is applause. You get into position.'

The Mayor, dressed in a suit, fur coat and chain of office, had stepped up to the podium. 'I have been looking forward, as Mayor and Chairman of the Electricity Committee, to switching on the Illuminations,' announced Alderman Whittaker, 'but after meeting Miss Mosson, I was very happy indeed to ask a queen to take my place.'

Gracie surveyed the crowd, hoping to spot Phyllis. There were so many people that she felt dizzy. Once or twice she saw one of them wave, and for a second, she hoped it was the maid, but it never was.

The spectators were applauding. Gracie could just make out Audrey in ceremonial robes at the side of the stage. The deep purple material embellished with thick golden thread in zigzags ran down her front like braces, each ending in a rose and tassel. The Railway Queen's eyes twinkled as she walked across to the podium.

Gracie swallowed the lump in her throat, Presto's gloating swam in her head again. 'I place the tiara in a black velvet bag. There is a great flash of light – a power overload. The electric bulbs shatter. The audience is plunged into darkness. When the lights come on, the tiara and I are gone. I have used the same routine in theatres all over England. It never fails.'

Was he right? Or could there still be a chance that Phyllis, Tom and Violet would be able to capture Presto? Even if it also meant Gracie found guilty for being his assistant?

Gracie glanced back at the church to her right. The minute hand was inching towards the twelve, ready to strike the hour.

'Ten . . .' began the crowd.

'Nine . . .'

'Eight . . .' Someone was pushing their way through the crowd.

People were squirming and stepping aside.

'Seven ...' She hoped it was Phyllis, George or Ma.

'Six ...'

'Five ...' She'd lost sight of them, and of hope of rescue.

'Four ...'

'Three ...'

'Two ...'

Audrey stepped proudly towards the white and gold Switch-On column.

'I hope the Blackpool Illuminations will illuminate the path of peace which the League of Nations is so nobly following on behalf of all young people throughout the world,' she said. 'May they symbolize industrial and international peace.'

'One ...'

The clock struck seven. Audrey pressed the large chrome button. The panel of lights around the main entrance and the town's motto of *Progress* suddenly burst into life, high above the heads of the crowd.

According to Violet, that was the signal for workmen at several substations along the prom to turn on their section. In just two minutes, all five miles of tableaux and lights would be illuminated.

Gracie watched as strings of bulbs stretched from lamppost to lamppost burst into white light, like a spider's web twinkling with morning dew.

It was strange how in such brightness everything felt so dark.

***

Presto stepped up to the podium, flicking his tuxedo tails out. He raised his arms to silence the applause. 'Thank you for such a generous welcome. Blackpool has always been very special to me. I first came here when I was just sixteen. I was staying in a small boarding house, down by the Pleasure Beach. I fell in love that holiday, with conjuring, with Blackpool and with a girl.'

'Aww,' sighed the crowd.

'Perhaps *you* are here with your girl?' he waved his arm in a sweeping gesture across the crowd. 'When you have a sweetheart, you treat her like a princess,' he let his arm flow towards Audrey. 'Or a Queen.'

'Miss Mosson, may I borrow your tiara?'

Gracie stepped forward. She could feel the audience's gaze move from Audrey to her. A shiver ran down her spine – she had never felt so exposed.

She realized the Railway Queen was staring too. She gave a slight nod and Audrey passed the tiara to Presto.

Spots of rain splashed on to the platform. Gracie moved closer to the Switch-On switch.

'I have here an ordinary velvet bag,' he held it up for the audience to see.

There was movement in the crowd. She could see people stand on their tiptoes, children swaying on their father's shoulders, but there was something else. Grunting and pushing; there was some kind of disturbance nearer the front.

It was Phyllis! *She must be moving in ready to catch Presto*, thought Gracie.

'I place the tiara in the bag . . .'

Gracie leaned forward ready to yank out the leads that fed into the base of the Switch-On switch column.

'. . . and Hey Presto!'

She closed her eyes and waited for the crowd's reaction to being plunged into darkness.

A hand suddenly gripped her own.

Gracie opened her eyes. It was Presto's. He was stopping her from turning off the lights.

He opened the bag, to show it was now empty. Then he lifted off his top hat and revealed the tiara.

'Oh, how clever,' said Audrey Mosson, clapping.

Presto smiled and passed the tiara back to the Railway Queen.

'It's just a cheap bit of costume jewellery,' he hissed.

***

Mr Emberton stepped towards the podium. 'The Mayor and his special guest, Miss Mosson, will now take a horse-drawn carriage promenade along the seafront to admire the animated tableaux,' he announced.

He beckoned to Violet and Tom, who stepped forward with a large wooden box.

Mr Emberton lifted out a huge glistening silver ceremonial mace. It was almost as tall as his children and was embossed with red, purple and pink precious stones.

Presto's eyes lit up like light bulbs.

Chapter Nineteen
One More Trick

'Violet! Tom!' Gracie called, but her voice was lost in the noise of the crowd. It was hopeless. Her friends were concentrating on handing the heavy mace over to the Mayor, who gave a final wave before escorting Audrey off stage.

'Let go off me!' cried Gracie, but Presto's grip tightened as he pulled her away from the dispersing crowd.

'Ow! You're hurting my arm.'

'Hey mister, geroff her,' said a scrawny-looking boy with curly hair.

'Mind your own business. Unless you want a thick ear.'

The boy raised his head proudly. Then he raised his arm high in the air. Gracie thought he was going to wallop Presto – but instead, he stared at her and clenched his hand open and shut making a signal like a shining star.

Presto huffed and tried to grab her arm again. There was just time for Gracie to make the signal back to the boy, before she was dragged away.

Gracie kicked out hard, catching Presto in the shin as he tried to pull her towards the carriage. He cursed but did not let go.

'You'll pay for that,' he dragged her across the tramlines towards the floodlit cenotaph where Alderman Whittaker and Audrey were getting into a horse-drawn carriage.

'Where are we going?' cried Gracie. 'Listen, I did what you asked. You have to let us all go. It's not my fault the tiara wasn't real.'

He was staring at the Mayor. 'I'm not bothered about that bit of tat. That mace, on the other hand, *is* worth having. Silver gilt with amethysts, carbuncles and corals – why, it must be the finest in the country!'

'Sadly, that mace is getting into a carriage,' Gracie retorted.

'That's not a problem, luckily I have pre-arranged transport.'

Parked just behind them was the Mayor's posh black car. The chauffeur was leaning against the bonnet, a peaked cap pulled down over his eyes.

The carriage passed the line of green beach shelters and along Princess Parade.

'Give me the car keys,' ordered Presto. The chauffeur looked up.

It wasn't a man.

It was Mrs Preston!

She tossed the keys to him and walked around to the passenger side. 'What happened to your signal? The lights didn't go out, so I didn't create the power surge.'

'Change of plan, darling. The tiara was cheap metal and glass, however, it's not all bad news. The Mayor has a priceless mace. So, we're taking a little diversion.' Presto yanked open the back door and pushed Gracie towards it. 'Get in.'

There was a muffled cry from inside the car.

'George?' she called, peering in.

'Gracie, help me, please,' he sobbed.

'I said, GET IN!'

Gracie moaned and slid on to the leather seat as Presto got behind the wheel and started up the engine.

Her brother's face was streaked with tears, and his nose was running. 'I'm sorry, Gracie. I was desperate for a wee, so I asked Tom if I could go to the loo. We thought it would be safe if he was watching Presto. We didn't know Mrs Preston had come back.'

'It doesn't matter.' She passed him Ma's hanky. 'Blow, George.' He sounded like an elephant. 'We're going to be all right,' said Gracie.

'Where are they taking us?' asked George.

'We're going for a little drive to the Cliffs,' said Presto. 'When we catch up with the Mayor, my wife will explain there's a problem with the car.

'While Alderman Whittaker is distracted, I'll grab Miss Mosson. Your sister will take her place. One teenager looks much like another, even Gracie could pass for the Railway Queen if we cover up her arm with that ceremonial robe. Then Gracie will ask the Mayor if she may take a closer look at the mace. Then – she'll give it to me.'

'I won't do it,' said Gracie. 'You can throw me off the Cliffs for all I care,' but there was a shaking to her voice which betrayed her lie.

'You will do it,' said Presto, 'or I'll throw your brother off the Cliffs.'

Gracie looked to George. She met his eyes so he would know she would never let that happen. She then noticed something wriggling in his jacket.

He placed a hand over it to keep it still. He'd brought his pet rat with him!

Ma's words rang in her head. *You should have left him in Milltown.* They should all have stayed in Milltown.

Gracie looked back at Talbot Square. The crowd was dispersing. For the first time in her life, she wished she was surrounded by people.

The car continued north, past the white colonnade and the sunken gardens and towards the end of the Illuminations. The whole area was deserted; there was no one to signal to for help.

'So, you only pretended to leave your husband,' said Gracie to Mrs Preston. 'You've been his loyal assistant all along. You both wanted Ma out of the way so she wouldn't alert the police to your con tricks.'

'How clever of you to work it out. A conjurer is always several steps ahead of his audience,' said Mrs Preston.

'It was you that called the police,' Gracie realised. 'You knew Ma wasn't in the cabinet any longer . . .'

Gracie rubbed her forehead, trying to work it out. Fred was squirming in George's jacket again. *Of course, he can't breathe!* she thought, as she suddenly remembered the holes in her brother's suitcase.

'Ma was in your suitcase! That's how you got her out of The Majestic.'

'You really do have a gift for working illusions out,' said Presto. 'I wish you would consider joining our act.'

Mrs Preston frowned.

Gracie sank back in her seat as the car curved back on to the main road. She had to stop Presto.

The roundabout was straight ahead. To Gracie's left was the first of the huge animated tableaux – pictures of fairy tales that seemed to move as the lights flicked on and off.

The car started to accelerate. This was her chance. Gracie leaned forward, wrapping her right arm around Presto's eyes.

George was pulling something out of his pocket. He leaned

forward and dropped Fred into Mrs Preston's lap. 'Urrgh, a rat!' she cried, flinging her arms up and hitting the side of her husband's head.

Presto gave an awful roar and steered crazily to the left. The car bumped up over the kerb and on to the path.

'Brake! Brake!' shouted Mrs Preston. 'We're all going to die!'

There was a screeching sound as Presto tried to bring the car under control.

'We're going to crash!' cried Mrs Preston. 'Peter, STOP!'

The car shot up on to the upper promenade, sliding on the wet ground towards the top of the Cliffs.

Chapter Twenty
To The Cliffs

The car smashed into another huge illumination tableaux. Gracie shielded her head at the sound of splintering wood and exploding lamps.

Gracie checked George first. He looked a bit dazed, but then a silly grin spread over his face. 'That was amazing! Like summat in a film!'

He was fine, but Gracie could see a large bruise forming on her right arm. She was also a bit shaky from both the adrenalin and the shock of what had just happened.

They had to get out. She began tugging desperately at the door handle. 'Come on, George – help me.'

Presto was groaning in the front. His head had smashed against the windscreen in the impact – a smear of blood on the glass marked the spot.

He opened the driver's door and clambered out.

The passenger side was wedged into the tableaux, which meant Mrs Preston had to crawl out after him.

Gracie's door would only open a bit. She shunted her body against the door from the inside, wincing at the pain to her bruised arm – and eventually it gave. She slid out of the back, followed by George and then slumped on to the ground, exhausted.

Suddenly, Presto lunged at her. 'You could have killed us!'

He shook Gracie like a rag doll.

George cowered against the wreck of the car, calling her name.

Gracie's ears were ringing. She could feel bile rising in her mouth. Had she ruptured an ear drum?

She closed her eyes and went limp, hoping that it would make Presto stop.

'Look,' called his wife.

The shaking stopped. Gracie sneaked a look.

Mrs Preston pointed down the Cliffs to the lower promenade where Audrey and the Mayor were now posing for photographs against the backdrop of the sea.

'The mace!' cried Presto. He released Gracie and she fell back against the rough ground.

'I'm coming too!' called his wife, hurrying after him.

The ringing in Gracie's ears was getting louder. Had she developed some kind of brain injury? She didn't recall banging her head, but maybe she'd blacked out.

'What's that noise?' asked George, now beside her.

Gracie stared. 'Can you hear it, an' all?'

'A bell,' they said together.

Gracie looked back towards Blackpool Tower and did a double take. There was a lifeboat on the tramlines and it was lit up in red, yellow and pink bulbs!

Violet and Tom were standing at the prow of the lifeboat, ringing a large ship's bell.

Behind them stood another twenty or so children, including one in an orange turban. They all raised their hands and signalled as they got nearer.

'It's an illuminated tram! Phyllis, Violet and Tom must have raised the alarm!' cried Gracie, her heart soaring. 'Look here comes another!' A double-decker tram with *PROGRESS* on the front and covered in thousands of lights pulled up behind.

'We're saved!' said George, as dozens of children piled off the trams and ran along the promenade.

Gracie hugged him, but over her shoulder she could see Presto and his wife heading for the Mayor. 'George, I need you to stay here. I'm going down to help Audrey.'

The path wound down through strange pink-brown rocks to the lower promenade. The wind buffeted against her legs as she descended.

Presto and his wife were running towards Audrey and the Mayor, who were admiring a tableaux with fairies on it.

The sea was wild. The smell of seaweed and brine made Gracie feel nauseous.

Halfway down, her foot slipped on a patch of slimy algae and she landed on her bottom. She snatched at tufts of wildflowers and sea grass as she tried to stand up.

Hot tears welled, but she would not be beaten. She shouted out, 'Audrey!'

The Railway Queen seemed to twitch. Had she heard?

Gracie could hear the roar of children, she glanced back, they were all clambering down the rocks.

Gracie made her way down the last stretch of path and sprinted towards the Railway Queen – her heart thumping.

Audrey hurled herself against Mrs Preston, her tiara flying off, then pinned her to the ground. She sat on top of her like a wrestler!

Peter Preston was grappling with the Mayor. He thumped Alderman Whittaker in the stomach, then wrenched the mace away from him.

Gracie picked up speed, she had to stop Presto!

She ran into the fracas, mouth open in a warrior scream – but the sound she heard was not her own.

It was a seagull! Her seagull!

The bird gave another terrifying cry and dive-bombed Presto, who tried to swipe at it with the mace. Gracie laughed as the seagull circled around him and released a trail of mess all over his head and shoulders.

Violet began shouting orders to the other kids. They formed a huge circle around the Prestons, blocking their escape. They held up their fists, ready for a punch-up if necessary.

Presto looked petrified. He glanced around for an escape route and clambered up on to the sea wall with the mace, striking out with it to keep the attackers at bay.

'Get down!' shouted Gracie. 'It's not safe!'

She could see the weight of the mace was causing him to wobble.

Audrey was dragging a dishevelled Mrs Preston towards them. The others were close behind.

'Drop it!' Gracie called.

'Not unless you let my wife go!' he cried.

Gracie steadied herself against a fierce gust. 'All right, Audrey release Mrs Preston. Everyone! Let Presto come down. He's going to surrender.'

The Railway Queen did as she was told, and Mrs Preston ran towards her husband.

'The mace, please,' said Gracie.

'I've changed my mind,' spat Presto, tottering on the wall.

'It's over,' wept his wife. 'Please come down.'

Gracie inched closer. She stretched out her hand. 'Give me the mace.'

'Never!' he cried, as a huge wave broke over the sea wall.

Presto toppled backwards, and was caught full force.

Gracie sprang back as she was sprayed with white foam. She gasped for breath and wiped her face and eyes.

'Peter!' wailed Mrs Preston.

The beautiful mace was lying by Gracie's feet. She picked it up, and then edged towards the sea wall.

Gracie looked down into the brown water for any sign of Presto, but the conjurer had disappeared.

Chapter Twenty-One

Applause

Gracie passed platefuls of hotpot around the kitchen table to Ma, George, Phyllis, Audrey, Violet and Tom, then sat down to eat. She stuck a spoon into the thick suet crust to let the steam out.

As they ate, the gang took it in turns to fill in the gaps as to what had happened.

'Poor Peter,' said Ma. 'I know he did some awful things – but he didn't deserve to die like that.'

'It was his own doing,' said Gracie. 'He could have stopped at any time.'

'He was a greedy man and he got his comeuppance,' said Audrey.

'It's Mrs Preston I feel sorry for,' said Tom.

'I know,' said Violet. 'Fancy her going back to Presto after the way he treated her!'

'I can't help feeling that could have been *me* facing a long prison sentence,' said Ma quietly, 'if I had made a different choice all those years ago.'

They were all quiet for a moment, lost in their thoughts.

'Thank goodness you were able to make the signal, Gracie,' said Phyllis. 'You should have seen it, all those kids, arms outstretched, making the sign of the Shining Star. It spread across the crowd like a wave. Then Violet and Tom told their pa to go and rescue your ma while everyone else commandeered the trams and went zooming down to the Cliffs!'

'The hardest part was convincing Violet she shouldn't drive,' said Tom, with a wink.

'We're sure to get a mention on Auntie Astra's page if nothing else,' said Violet, grinning. 'I think Pa's quite impressed now he knows Tom and I helped you save the day, although he's still determined to keep the whole story out of the Gazette; he doesn't want any bad publicity about the Switch-On. After all, he's hoping it'll happen again next year, and for years to come.'

'They might even ask you to do it again, Audrey. You did a brilliant job,' said Tom.

'You were even better at wrestling Mrs Preston!' added George.

'Still, Mrs Preston put up a pretty good fight when that policeman tried to arrest her,' said Phyllis.

'Never mind her. It's you two I'm worried about,' said Ma, wrinkles appearing on her brow. 'You're sure you're not hurt?'

'Just a few scrapes and bruises,' said Gracie. 'Mrs Preston wasn't keen on me taking Mrs Hill's necklace back.' She held up the pendant.

'Me and Fred are fine an' all,' said George, offering his pet rat a piece of crust. 'Do you think we'll get a reward for saving the Mayor's mace?' he asked. 'I think Fred would like a medal.'

'I thought we'd agreed that your keeping Presto's doves, rabbits *and* Sunny the budgie was enough of a reward,' said Gracie.

'I suppose,' said George. He gave a big smile. 'We could be an animal boarding house an' all from now on!'

'There's no better reward than having your family all together again,' said Ma. 'Although I suppose you dislike Blackpool more than ever, after all the trouble we've had.'

'Oh, not at all,' said Gracie. 'We've made new friends and visited the pier, the Tower and the Pleasure Beach – just like you did on your childhood holidays.'

Ma's face was full of hope as she looked at her children.

'However, we would like to make a few changes to The Majestic' said Gracie.

'I suppose the place could do with modernizing,' said Ma.

'We could decorate the place during the winter season, when it's quiet.'

Gracie smiled. 'I think children should be able to have a Full English for breakfast, like the adults do.'

'Hmm,' said Ma. 'Well, I could charge more for the extra bacon and eggs . . . Go on, agreed.'

'Also, Phyllis has to have a permanent job here at The Majestic,' said Gracie, smiling at the maid.

'Absolutely, and she can have a raise,' said Ma.

'Oh, that's wonderful!' said Phyllis.

Ma looked hopefully at Gracie and George. 'So – you *do* like it here in Blackpool? You want to stay on at The Majestic?'

George lifted his pet rat to his ear. 'Fred says yes. He likes Blackpool.'

'So do I,' said Gracie, grinning. 'In fact, I love it. I want to stay forever.'

THE END

GLOSSARY

ALDERMAN – The title given to the Mayor of Blackpool. There have been over 100 Aldermen, including John Bickerstaffe who built Blackpool Tower.

AMELIA EARHART – An American aviator who set many flying records including becoming the first woman to fly solo across the Atlantic Ocean.

ANIMATED TABLEAUX – Large pictures made up of different coloured lamps that give the illusion of movement when turned on and off.

ANTIMACASSER – Cloths (sometimes lace) that are placed over the backs and arms of chairs and settees. They were originally designed to stop men's hair oil from damaging the furniture.

BALUSTRADE – A small row of columns topped by a rail on a staircase or terrace.

BARM CAKE – A soft bread roll that is popular with people in the North West of England, especially when filled with chips!

BLACKPOOL CLIFFS – Man-made rocks constructed in 1922 by James Pulham & Sons.

BLACKPOOL GAZETTE – The Gazette began life as a weekly newspaper in 1873 and was started by Alderman John Grime. The Gazette became a daily/evening newspaper in 1929 and has also been known as the West Lancashire Gazette.

BLACKPOOL MACE – This silver gilt ornamental staff or

walking stick was presented to Blackpool to mark Queen Victoria's Diamond Jubilee.

BLACKPOOL PIERS – Blackpool has three Victorian piers – North, Central and South. These platforms on pillars stretch from the shore to the sea and were designed as entertainment attractions.

BLACKPOOL ROCK – Made by boiling and pulling sugar, this traditional sweet with letters in the middle is believed to have been sold in Blackpool since the 1880s.

BLACKPOOL TOWER – Blackpool Tower opened to the public on 14th May 1894, it was inspired by the Eiffel Tower in Paris. Although it has changed internally over time, some key features survive including the Tower Ballroom, the Tower Circus and the Tower Ascent.

BLACKPOOL TOWER MENAGERIE – A collection of wild animals that were put on exhibition for the public from 1873-1973.

BLANCMANGE – A wobbly, sweet milk jelly made with cream, milk and sugar.

BOARDING HOUSE – An old-fashioned name for a guest house or B&B.

CHAMBERPOT – A portable ceramic pot kept in a bedroom to be used as a toilet during the night. Sometimes called a gazunder (because it was kept under the bed) or a jerry.

CLOCHE HAT – A fitted, bell-shaped hat made of felt, worn by ladies. Popular in the 1920s and early 1930s.

CONJURER – Someone who performs magic tricks, also known as a magician.

DECCA GRAMOPHONE – A record player made by the British company 'Decca'.

ECCLES CAKES – A delicious flaky pastry cake made with currants and topped with sugar.

EMPORIUM – A large shop that sells a range of goods.

ESPLANADE – A paved area next to the sea for walking.

FESTOON – The term given to strings of lights.

FRED ASTAIRE – A Hollywood actor, singer and dancer who was best known for his dancing partnership with actress Ginger Rogers.

FUN HOUSE – One of Blackpool Pleasure Beach's fairground attractions that opened in 1934. It was sadly destroyed in a fire in 1991.

HANGAR – A very large open building often for storing aircraft and other types of transport.

HIRAM MAXIM'S FLYING MACHINE – Blackpool Pleasure Beach's oldest fairground ride named after its inventor who designed an early aircraft. It was created in 1904 and is still in operation today.

HOTPOT – A traditional Lancashire dish made of lamb or mutton and onions, then topped with sliced potato.

HOUDINI – A famous magician and escapologist.

LANDLADY – The owner and manager of a boarding house who would often have house rules that set out what was allowed and not allowed.

LAUGHING MAN – A mechanical figure bought by Leonard Thompson, owner of The Pleasure Beach, from the Galeries Lafeyette department store in Paris. The original head survived the Fun House fire in 1991.

LEAGUE OF THE SHINING STAR – The Lancashire Gazette newspaper's Blackpool Edition included a regular children's page called The League of the Silver Star written by Auntie Stella. Blackpool children were invited to send in letters and enter competitions, and would receive a certificate once they joined up.

LEGERDEMAIN / SLEIGHT OF HAND – Quick or deceptive movements of the hand used to perform conjuring tricks.

MÖBIOUS LOOP ROLLERCOASTER – A clever rollercoaster design named after a German mathematician.

OPEN AIR BATHS – The South Shore Open Air Baths was the largest open air swimming pool or lido in the world when it opened in 1923. The Miss Blackpool beauty pageants were often held here.

PARLOUR – A sitting room. A shared space for guests in a boarding house. In a private home often rarely used except on very special occasions.

PLEASURE BEACH – The amusement park or fairground was founded at South Shore in 1896 by Alderman William George Bean.

PONTOON – A card game in which players aim for a hand of five cards totalling 21 points or less.

PROPELLERS – The rotating blades on the nose of smaller or older aircraft.

RAILWAY QUEEN – Inspired by the tradition of Village Rose and May Queens, British Industries decided to 'elect' their own Queens.

REGINALD DIXON – Despite being known as 'Mr Blackpool', Reginald Dixon was actually from Sheffield, Yorkshire. He was hired to play the organ at the Blackpool Tower Ballroom for one season in 1930 and stayed in the job until his retirement in 1970!

ROCKETS SLOT MACHINE – A coin-operated amusements game. They were withdrawn because they were faulty and paid out too often.

SANDGROWN – Born and raised in Blackpool.

SHIRLEY TEMPLE – A 1930's Hollywood child star/actress.

SIDESHOW – Exhibits on the Golden Mile that often featured fortune tellers and animals. Customers were encouraged to pay to look at everything from waxworks to starving brides.

SWITCH-ON – A popular ceremony in which Blackpool's Illuminations are switched on for the year, usually by a guest of honour. The first official Illuminations Switch-On ceremony was conducted by Lord Derby in 1934.

THE GOLDEN MILE – The 1.7 mile stretch of promenade along the seafront between the North and South Piers. It is well known for its souvenir shops, amusement arcades and fish and chip shops.

TOWN HALL – The council offices on Talbot Square were built between 1895 and 1900. Blackpool's Switch-On ceremonies used to take place in front of the building before moving to the more spacious Pier Head.

TRAM – A passenger vehicle powered by electricity conveyed by overhead cables and running on rails laid in a public road. Blackpool has the oldest electric street tramway in the world.

TRAM DEPOT / ILLUMINATIONS DEPOT – The tram depot was built in 1935 for the storage and repair of Blackpool's trams, while the Illuminations depot is said to have been a former stable for beach donkeys!

VIRGINIA REEL – A Blackpool Pleasure Beach fairground ride that span passengers round as it twisted down a track on a steep slope. It opened in 1922 and was replaced 60 years later in 1982.

WINTER GARDENS – An entertainment complex in Blackpool town centre. It opened in 1878 and included a glass roof, an opera house and skating rinks.

WIRELESS – The original name for a radio.

WURLITZER ORGAN – Designed by Reginald Dixon himself, the Wurlitzer Organ is still a very popular attraction of the Blackpool Tower Ballroom, with large crowds regularly dancing to its unique sound. This iconic instrument rises out of the stage floor and has over 1000 pipes and 154 keys!

AUTHOR'S NOTE

Gracie Fairshaw and the Mysterious Guest is set in Blackpool in 1935 during the run-up to the Illuminations Switch-On ceremony.

The plot was inspired by my childhood daytrips to Blackpool in the 1980s. I have fantastic memories of visiting the Illuminations and Blackpool Tower, especially the aquarium, circus and the lift to the top. I also loved going to the Pleasure Beach. My favourite rides were Noah's Ark, River Caves, Alice in Wonderland and the Ghost Train.

I wanted to write a book that highlights Blackpool's incredible seaside heritage. I love writing historical fiction and I was keen to feature real people, real events and real places. When I discovered a fifteen-year-old girl – Audrey Mosson – was the second person to perform the Illuminations Switch-On ceremony, I knew I had the spark for my story.

I also wanted a heroine who reflected my upbringing; she too would be Northern and working class. Gracie Fairshaw was also inspired by my family. My mum uses a wheelchair but never lets her disability stop her from embracing life. Gracie was born with limb difference like my great grandfather who had his left arm amputated at the elbow during World War One.

The Majestic does not exist, although Osborne Road does. However, Blackpool had lots of boarding houses in the 1930s – nowadays known as 'guest houses' or 'B&Bs'.

The original boarding houses did not provide meals – some landladies however would cook dishes for guests if they provided the ingredients – for an extra charge! Soon visitors became accustomed to the idea of meals being included and landladies found it easier to buy their own supplies. Some landladies apparently charged for extras including use of salt and pepper (the cruets). Most boarding house rooms were simple with just a wash basin and a chamber pot, rather than the modern concept of an en-suite bathroom!

A lot of boarding houses guests would stay for a week. The day they left and new ones arrived was known as Changeover Day. The Blackpool Illuminations meant an extended visitor season, originally for thirty-one days, but now run from the end of August to the first week of November.

Miss Steele was inspired by the real-life Mass Observation Project. Actually formed in January 1937, observers studied ordinary working class people from Bolton, which was renamed 'Worktown' for the project.

Observers were interested in daily routine, diet and health pastimes. They even watched people on their holidays – and this meant lots of information was gathered about trips to Blackpool.

Blackpool is famous around the world for its Tower and the Illuminations. In the 1930s, despite Britain being in a depression, thousands of people spent their holidays in the resort. Many came for the beaches and its many entertainments.

These included three piers, the Winter Gardens complex and the Pleasure Beach.

The Hiram Maxim Flying Machine (1904) was originally located on the sands. As the fairground grew in the early 1920s, new attractions were added including a wooden rollercoaster named The Big Dipper, along with The Noah's Ark and the Virginia Reel.

Another transformation in the 1930s saw designer Joseph Emberton (whose name I borrowed for Violet and Tom) create more rides in a modern Art Deco style including the world's first Ghost Train, the Grand National and the Fun House.

The Noah's Ark building is no longer accessible but forms the entrance to the Pleasure Beach. The Flying Machines, the Big Dipper, the Ghost Train and the Grand National rides are still in operation.

In 1879 Blackpool's seafront was lit up by a row of eight electric arc lights on eighteen-metre high poles. Some people called electric light 'Electric Sunshine' as it was so much brighter than the oil lamps and candlelight in people's homes.

Electric lights were then used on five tram cars to celebrate Queen Victoria's Diamond Jubilee in 1897. When Princess Louise was invited to open the new Metropole Hotel in 1912, Tramways and Electrical Engineer Charles Furness suggested the council could make their own lights for the nearby Promenade. Strings of electric lamps were strung between lampposts, up flagpoles and in decorative arches. A new No.68 tram passed by with 3,000 lights on it – and was a huge hit with locals.

The Town Council decided they wanted more, and so the first Blackpool Illuminations began on September 8th 1912. A number of illuminated trams were built over the years including Gondola in 1925, Lifeboat, Progress and the Blackpool Belle.

The first Switch-On ceremony took place in 1934. In 1935, Alderman George Whittaker should have performed the Switch-On, but when he met Railway Queen Audrey Mosson, a Blackpool girl, he asked her to take his place.

Fifty years later, Audrey was again invited to perform the Switch-On ceremony, this time with actress Joanna Lumley.

I have thoroughly enjoyed carrying out research to help write my book. I have spent hours at the Blackpool Local History Library going through old newspaper cuttings. I have walked in Gracie's footsteps, have heard the Wurlitzer in the Tower Ballroom (where I have since learned my grandparents first met!) and taken the Tower Ascent. I have returned to the Pleasure Beach and ridden the Flying Machines and Grand National. I have watched a Blackpool Magic Show at the Horseshoe Bar, Pleasure Beach and ridden on a heritage tram. I have also visited South Pier and seen high tide at the Cliffs.

I have enjoyed behind the scenes tours at the Blackpool Tower, Blackpool Town Hall and the Lightworks depot – where

I saw illuminations being repaired. I was also able to have a photograph taken with the Switch-On column. I have even seen Audrey Mosson's Railway Queen gown and tiara at a museum in Leeds.

And of course, I have been to the Illuminations themselves and I was absolutely chuffed to win tickets to the 2018 Switch-On ceremony, where I saw Alfie Boe turn on the lights.

Long may the tradition continue!

ACKNOWLEDGEMENTS

Thank you to mum and dad for the trips to Blackpool and for letting me spend many, many hours with my head in a book, and for believing in me and my ambitions.

Karen, thanks for being a lovely sister and for going on all those rides at Blackpool with me as a kid!

Rachel, thanks for being my brilliant best friend and for exploring Blackpool with me!

Shout out to my SCBWI pals, especially the North West crit group and my co-organiser Catherine. Huge thanks to Mel, Anna, Faye, Jayne, Lois and Marion for your friendship, encouragement, patience and insightful manuscript feedback and suggestions. You guys rock!

I would also like to thank the SCBWI Undiscovered Voices team, and especially the fabulous Sara Grant for her advice and support.

Love to everyone at Norton Priory Museum, especially Allison and Claire for sorting out rotas and lieu days so I could attend crit group, write and research.

Thanks to the Blackpool Civic Trust and the History Centre, Blackpool and Lightworks for tours, advice and use of the microfiche reader.

Thank you to everyone at Uclan Publishing especially Hazel Holmes, Toni Murtagh and Charlotte Rothwell. A big thank you to Natalie Graham, Becca Grant and Bev Gilmour for championing my book and choosing it as your student project.

Jenny Czerwonka – thank you for the superb cover design and chapter head illustrations.

Thank you Kathy Webb for line edits.

A big cheer for everyone at Bounce and all the booksellers and reviewers who have supported my book.

Finally, Dan, thank you for all the cups of tea, putting up with the 'tippy-tapping' of my laptop keys, joining me on even more trips to Blackpool, and most of all for being a fabulous husband!

ABOUT THE AUTHOR

Susan Brownrigg is a Lancashire lass. She grew up in Wigan, lives in Skelmersdale and is obsessed with Blackpool. She works as a museum learning & community manager.

In 2015, Susan was awarded the Society of Children's Book Writers and illustrator's British Isles Margaret Carey Scholarship for fiction. She is also a SCBWI BI 2016 Undiscovered Voices competition winner.

This is a photograph of Susan with the original Switch-on button at Blackpool Illuminations Depot, Rigby Road, Blackpool, Lancashire.

IF YOU LIKE THIS, YOU'LL LOVE . . .

The first book in a new electrifying series
from author of *Sky Thieves*, Dan Walker.

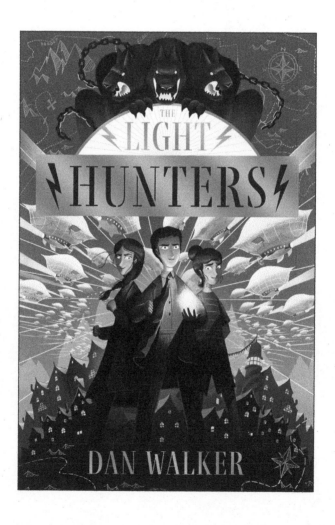

Dare you travel to Inchtinn – where sinister beings stir and tormented souls seek revenge? What if survival relies on facing your greatest fears?

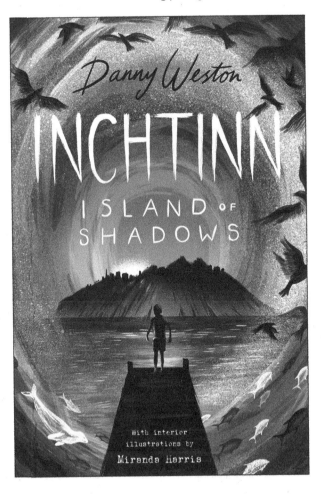

Danny Weston

INCHTINN

ISLAND OF SHADOWS

With interior
illustrations by
Miranda Harris

The first book in a gripping new fantasy
adventure series from New York Times
bestselling author A. J. Hartley.

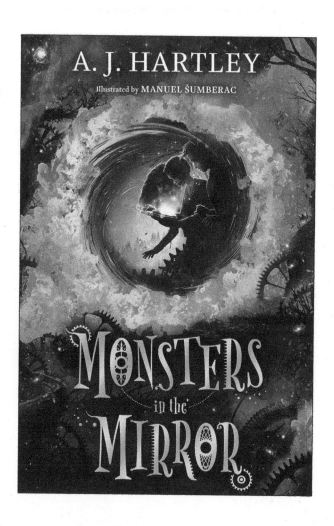

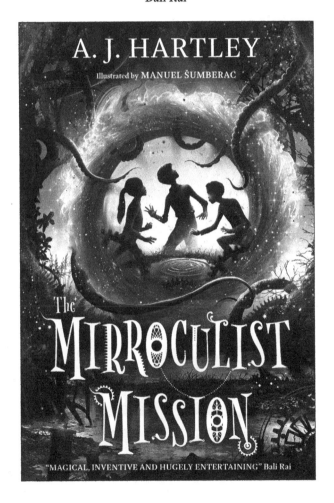

A. J. HARTLEY

Illustrated by MANUEL ŠUMBERAC

The
MIRROCULIST
MISSION

A rollicking medieval romp where laughter
and action abound in equal measure...
And where danger lurks around every corner.

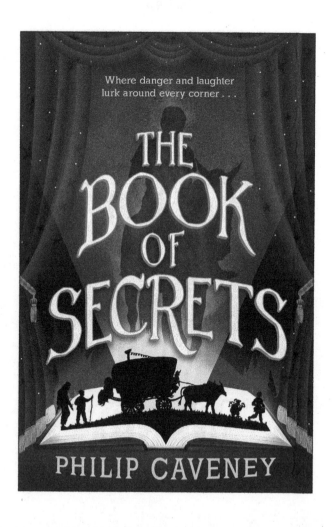

Where danger and laughter
lurk around every corner . . .

THE
BOOK
OF
SECRETS

PHILIP CAVENEY

Revamped new edition of the bestselling VAMPIRATES series, with new exclusive content added!

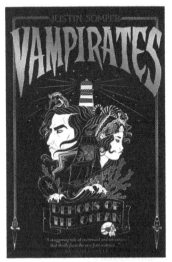

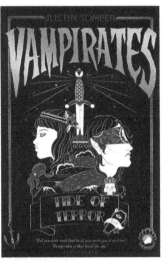

HAVE YOU EVER WONDERED
HOW BOOKS ARE MADE?

UCLan Publishing are based in the North of England and involve BA Publishing and MA Publishing students from the University of Central Lancashire at every stage of the publishing process.

BA Publishing and MA Publishing students are based within our company and work on producing books as part of their course – some of which are selected to be published and printed by UCLan Publishing. Students also gain first-hand experience of negotiating with buyers, conceiving and running innovative high-level events to leverage sales, as well as running content creation business enterprises.

Our approach to business and teaching has been recognised academically and within the publishing industry. We have been awarded Best Newcomer at the Independent Publishing Guild Awards (2019) and a *Times* Higher Education Award for Excellence and Innovation in the Arts(2018).

As our business continues to grow, so too does the experience our students have upon entering UCLan Publishing.

To find out more, please visit
www.uclanpublishing.com/courses/